GUNS BLAZE
AT SUNDOWN

GUNS BLAZE
AT SUNDOWN

AL CODY

WHEELER
CHIVERS

This Large Print edition is published by Wheeler Publishing, Waterville, Maine, USA and by AudioGO Ltd, Bath, England.
Wheeler Publishing, a part of Gale, Cengage Learning.
Copyright © 1952 by Archie Joscelyn.
Copyright © renewed 1980 by Archie Joscelyn.
The moral right of the author has been asserted.

LIBRARY OF CONGRESS CATALOGING-IN-PUBLICATION DATA	
Cody, Al, 1899–1986. 　Guns blaze at sundown / by Al Cody. — Large print ed. 　　p. cm. — (Wheeler Publishing large print western) 　ISBN-13: 978-1-4104-3981-9 (pbk.) 　ISBN-10: 1-4104-3981-X (pbk.) 　1. Large type books. I. Title. PS3519.O712G78 2011 813'.54—dc22	2011017529

BRITISH LIBRARY CATALOGUING-IN-PUBLICATION DATA AVAILABLE

Published in 2011 in the U.S. by arrangement with Golden West Literary Agency.
Published in 2012 in the U.K. by arrangement with Golden West Literary Agency.

U.K. Hardcover: 978 1 445 83844 1 (Chivers Large Print)
U.K. Softcover: 978 1 445 83845 8 (Camden Large Print)

Printed in the United States of America
1 2 3 4 5 6 7 15 14 13 12 11

CONTENTS

CONTENTS

PRINCIPAL CHARACTERS

Tom Shannon He inherited a cattle empire — and a bullet in the back from the man who wanted his ranch.

Thad Gormley The local doctor — who had been run out of town when one of his patients died — under mysterious circumstances.

Nancy Adams She packed guns as well as any man — but she became a woman when she looked at Tom.

Judge Weldon Broken in spirit by the death of his daughter, he was easy prey to the evil schemes of the man who had stolen Tom's ranch.

Bill Pesky An untypical sheriff — short, stocky, quiet looking. His lightning guns and honesty made him many friends — and enemies.

Waldron Cowles He thought he had found the perfect setup when he bushwhacked Tom and took over his ranch — till a "corpse" with blazing guns changed his mind.

■ ■ ■ ■

PART I
"GET OUT OF
TOWN, STRANGER!"

■ ■ ■ ■

ONE

Twice unseen death had barely missed Shannon in the last seventy hours. This third time, apparently, was the charm; his luck had run out. He was too late to avoid the smashing impact of a high-powered bullet, but quick enough to partially spoil the killer's aim. Not that he could guess it, then.

The flight of a bird saved his life. A magpie, handsome scavenger of the northern latitudes, came coasting on an air current, wings scarcely moving, heading towards a clump of boulders. There were half a dozen of these, big as wagons, which the sun and wind had freed of the encompassing snow. The magpie was settling gracefully toward one of them when with sudden wild beat of wings it changed course and headed off at right angles. The sharp crack of the rifle sounded a moment later.

Shannon's eyes, as he rode, had caught sight of the bird, beautiful in its flashing black and white against the blue of sky above and snowy white earth below. Seeing it swerve, he knew that it had discovered something alien there among the boulders and clustering brush — maybe a coyote or weasel, perhaps a more potent enemy, such as had been seeking his own life these last few days.

His gaze dropped in time to catch the sheen of sunlight along a rifle-barrel as it moved slightly, and Shannon touched his horse with the spurs, started to fling himself to the side in the same instant.

The bullet hit like a giant's kick, shock coursing through his whole body as the lead tore its way, driving him backward out of the saddle. Smashing gun-thunder rang in his ears and then was muted and lost as pain flooded over him. He was falling. . . .

There was confusion of pain, long darkness which smothered, partial awakenings in which he tried to struggle up to life and light and was dragged down again. Actual wakening, when it came, was another shock, though of lesser degree.

Shannon opened his eyes, fuzzily aware that his head felt wrong and that his left side and shoulder hurt. For that matter, there was an ache in most of his body, a sick dizziness which went all through him.

But out of the miasma emerged a strangely friendly face, swimming somewhere between floor and ceiling — a face with sharp blue eyes and high cheekbones and a curious tuft of brownish hair which refused to stay in place.

A voice said something soothing and re-assuring. Memory, nagging at the corners of Shannon's consciousness, gave up the struggle, and he drifted off to sleep again.

That was like part of a dream when he awoke again. His head was clearer, but there was still pain and a sick feeling. He looked around, while blurred objects slowly came into focus. Then, as he made sure that he was awake, he began to wonder if he might not still be dreaming.

It should be winter — with rivers ice-locked and the land sheathed in snow. Yet a meadow-lark was singing, close at hand, the notes pure and joyous as in nesting-time. He saw it then, with yellow waistcoat and black necktie, perched near-by.

Overhead, a blue-bird preened its feathers. That log on which it sat was a beam, for there was ceiling above. Now arose a familiar chattering and scolding as a red squirrel raced between the two birds.

Shannon blinked. Then, while he tried to order his thoughts, a door opened, and with it there swirled a blast of wintry air, quickly gone as the door closed again. Then came the man with the twinkling blue eyes. He was stripping off mittens, revealing himself as youthful as Shannon, though more slightly built.

Snow lingered on his shoulders, but the blue-bird hopped to light on one of them. The squirrel raced to the floor and then frisked up a leg and into a capacious coat pocket. It popped back out indignantly as a wood-mouse also stuck its head out of the pocket.

Bewildered, Shannon wondered if he was really awake. But now, seeing his eyes open, the other man approached, smiling warmly.

"So you're taking an interest in life again, my friend? Good!" He laid a hand on Shannon's forehead for a moment, nodded reassuringly. "No fever — or very little! You're coming along fine."

"What happened?" Shannon asked, and was surprised to find his voice a croak, scarcely above a whisper.

His host removed his coat and hung it on a peg, carefully removing the mouse first. He crossed to a stove in a corner of the room and stuffed in more wood, then turned back.

"Nothing to worry about — now," he said.

"Somebody took a shot at you. But you're going to be all right."

It came back to Shannon then. Those mysterious but unmistakable attempts on his life, over a trio of days. Then, with Vermillion only a few miles ahead, the coursing magpie, the gleam of a moving rifle. . . . So he had been shot. It was no dream.

"Yes, somebody put a bullet into you and left you for dead," the other man explained, rattling pots and pans, while the squirrel scampered excitedly and the blue-bird flew back to the rafter near the lark. "You were bloody and dead-looking enough, when I found you, to fool almost anyone. You even had me guessing, for a while."

He turned, with that quick, warm smile.

"But between us, you with your vitality, me with my small skill, we'll fool whoever it was. You'll be as good as ever, one of these fine days. And now I'll wager that you're hungry."

Shannon was. Ravenous, in fact. His host dished up a bowl of savory-smelling soup, then sat beside the bunk and spooned it out to Shannon as though he had been a baby.

"Quite a while since yesterday mornin' and breakfast," Shannon commented. "I was aimin' to get supper in Vermillion —"

"It wasn't yesterday," his host replied.

15

"I've managed to feed you a bit, now and then. But you've been a very sick man, my friend. For quite a while. Out of your head, or sunk in a coma. It was touch and go for a while."

Shannon considered that. So it hadn't been all a bad dream, after all.

"How long?" he asked.

"Approximately three weeks."

Three weeks in which he had hovered between life and death, surviving only because of this Good Samaritan's care. But now, thanks to that care and skill at healing, he was definitely on the road to recovery.

"Sick creatures seem to get well here," his new friend explained, on the following day. "That squirrel had been so unlucky as to find himself in the claws of an owl, and was just about dead when I rescued him. The blue-bird had a broken leg, the lark was in pitiful condition. Ants had found the nest, with the half-grown birds in it — just too small to fly or escape. I saved this youngster, and he's been doing very well for himself since. There was a deer, for a while — and even myself."

He fell silent, as if considering that last remark.

"Mental illness can be worse than physical, at times. I don't mean what we term

16

insanity, but that which may be as bad — depression. But this is a healing land, when you give it a chance. I'm Thad Gormley," he added. "And I suppose, if they knew about this, in Vermillion, they'd hate me more than ever."

"Hate you? How so? For what?" Shannon demanded.

"I don't usually bore company by talking about myself," Gormley said lightly. "Forget it."

"But I'd like to know," Shannon insisted.

"Sure of that? Well — all right. It's a relief to talk about it. You see, I used to call myself a medico — a doctor. I even had a fairly good practice, there in Vermillion, up to half a year ago." He was talking in an unemotional voice, smiling faintly, but Shannon saw the shadow of pain in his eyes, and he had a hunch that this recital was a part of the doctor's stern treatment of his own case. That he was talking now, deliberately, about something which he would have preferred to keep buried. Forcing himself to discuss it casually, as a part of his own cure.

"Yes, I was the doctor there. And I figured myself as being pretty good, for a country practitioner. Maybe I wasn't. Not too good, anyway. For a patient of mine — died. It was something I couldn't help. God knows

I tried!"

His voice had grown husky, sharp with pain. He stared unseeingly at the frost-rimmed window, went on.

"They said that I poisoned her! Whether by mistake, or deliberately, there was at least a difference of opinion. Some of them imputed the worst possible motives to me. But everyone was stirred up. They called me a quack, which wasn't so good. But when they called me a murderer — and for the reasons they gave — that hurt."

He blinked rapidly, absent-mindedly stroking the squirrel, which had jumped on to his knee.

"A murderer — when I'd have given my own heart's-blood to have saved her! But she died. And they told me to get out of town. In fact, they even gave me a ride out — on a rail. With the warning that if I ever showed my face there again, they'd lynch me!"

Gormley smiled sadly. "She was just a young girl — about nineteen. At the threshold of life. Everybody loved her. I knew how they felt.

"Well, I took the hint. I've been living here, deep in these hills, back on this side of the river, for over half a year. I doctor a few wild things. It's something to practice on,

18

and they, at least, are grateful. That's the story. And you are getting well, though it will be quite a while before you have your strength back. They'd be surprised, if they knew I was still in this country. When I need supplies, I go to Twin Buttes."

Twin Buttes. That was down river on the opposite side from Vermillion. Shannon had spent his last night there, before being shot. Someone had taken a shot at him there, from the darkness.

Gormley was a friendly soul, starving for companionship. Shannon warmed to him, shocked at the tragedy of the doctor's life. He liked him increasingly when he learned that Gormley had looked around until he found his horse, and had brought it back and cared for it also. As to the shooting, he professed to have no theories on the subject.

"But why should anyone want to kill me?" Shannon wondered. "I'm a stranger in this part of the country. Never been around here before. I was headin' for Thunder River Ranch. And I guess I haven't even told you my name. It's Shannon. Tom Shannon."

Gormley reached to shake hands gravely.

"I'm glad to know you, Tom. Thunder River Ranch, eh?"

"Yes. Do you know it?"

"I've been there. A good ranch. . . . . You

19

were headin' there to look for a job?"

"Not exactly. Maybe I'd better give you a little personal history, since you've told me about yourself. I've always been a cowboy — sort of fiddle-footed. Never been much of a hand to stay long in any one place. I'd always get to wonderin' what was over the next hill. So, when I get any mail, which don't happen often, it sometimes takes it a long time to catch up with me. But along here a spell back, a letter did come — one that had been near half a year in tryin' to. It was from a lawyer in a little town called Poncas.

"Dwyer was his name. Sylvester Dwyer. Friendly sort of a chap. To finally get around to answerin' your question, he told me that an uncle of mine that I'd never seen, Bart Redding, had died, leaving me his ranch. Thunder River Ranch, up beyond Vermillion."

"Bart Redding?" Gormley exclaimed. "Was he your uncle? I knew him well. Mighty nice fellow."

"That so? Well, you can imagine how surprised I was. I'd never known that I had any relations that had any money, much less a big ranch. And the notion that Uncle Bart would leave anything to me, a nephew he'd set eyes on only once, back when I was a baby — that was even more surprisin'." Shannon found it easy to confide in this friendly, lonely man to whom he owed his life.

"Life is full of surprises," Gormley nodded. "And some of them are pleasant. If you're the owner of Thunder River Ranch, you're fortunate. It's a fine place."

"That's what Mr. Dwyer said. Big, free of debt, and well-stocked with the best cattle in this part of the state. He turned all the papers over to me, once I had convinced him that I was the real Tom Shannon and the legal heir. I was lucky about that."

"How do you mean?"

"Lucky to be able to show him who I was. I just happened to have some old papers that showed who I was, or there wouldn't have been any way to prove I was Uncle Bart's nephew. Well, after I got things fixed up, I started for the ranch." He paused. "Somebody tried to kill me along the way — three different times. But why, is more'n I can figure out."

Gormley's face was grave.

"Were you carryin' those papers, when you were shot?"

"Why, yes. I knew I'd have to show 'em to the foreman and mebbe some other local folks. You mean —"

"There were no papers of any sort on you when I found you," Gormley said. "Nothing. You'd been left for dead. And, from the looks of things, robbed."

Two

Shannon considered that, frowning, then shook his head.

"Anybody that robbed me, sure didn't get much," he said. "Dwyer offered me some money, but I preferred to get along till I got to the ranch. As for the papers — well, I'd written to Uncle Bart's foreman that I was comin.' He'll be wonderin' what's delayed me, but that won't make much difference."

"You wrote him a letter yourself — in your own writing?"

"Why, sure. How else?"

Gormley sighed with relief.

"That makes it all right, then. If he's hard to convince, he can compare your handwriting with that letter."

"Yeah. And if he wanted to be cautious, Dwyer could soon set it straight. . . . But what worries me is about you. You've had a raw deal. When I get settled up there, I'm going to try and make up to you for what you've done for me, as far as I can. I'll sure tell folks in Vermillion what a set of fools

22

they've made of themselves."

Gormley shook his head.

"I appreciate your intentions, Tom," he said. "But I prefer it this way. Let them think that I'm dead, or long gone from Montana. I'm well satisfied with the life I'm living. There's nothing up there that appeals to me, now. With them fightin' over the Dusky Lady — that's a mine — and all sorts of trouble —" he shrugged. "I don't want any of it."

Shannon's recovery was rapid. But it was some time before he was back to normal, and Gormley insisted that he remain with him until he felt fit. But there came a day when he could delay no longer, and bade his friend good-bye, with a promise to return and see him.

Nothing bothered today. Ice covered Thunder River, and he crossed on that, to Vermillion, a county seat cow-town which in the last few years was taking on a new aspect as it became somewhat of a mining center. The Big C mine was off a few miles, with a dozen shafts boring into the earth, the hoists bringing up ore with clock-like regularity. Ore containing a bit of silver, some copper, and a lot of gold. Other shafts were continually being sunk, in feverish activity, while litigation with a rival mine, the Dusky Lady, kept interest at a feverish pitch. Gormley had told him about it.

Mines held no particular interest for Shannon. Just enough of the mining interest could be seen from the town to whet the interest. Closer at hand but still on the outskirts was the court house, a building of native stone, big and impressive. It was set on a rise of ground, flanked by big-gaunt-branched cottonwoods, with Thunder River off at the side.

The town was busy today, probably because the weather had turned suddenly pleasant. Snow melted in the sun, the streets were sloppy. Shannon pushed through and on, north and a little west, following the river. Impatience quickened in him. Hills arose, darkly timbered but frosted with the snow. Hills which gave way to mountains that sawed the sky-line into ragged edges. The river made a wide curving U at the town, and it did the same again as he approached the ranch.

On this eastern shore the valley narrowed. The slopes were steep, with shaggy pines shutting away the sun, crowding into the meadows. They hung, bearded with moss, ghostly in a giant aloofness.

Then he saw the home buildings. A huge log house, tall as well as wide, dominated the cluster of lesser dwellings, which stood close to it as if for protection. Big barns and corrals were at one side. A shoulder of hill jutted at the rear of the house, topped by mighty pines.

Several men, lounging or at work, looked up curiously at his approach. One man moved with an air of conscious authority, so that Shannon judged he must be the foreman. He was an inch short of six feet, with dark hair above a smoothly shaven face, the iron look of whiskers showing beneath taut skin. He stood, feet wide apart, waiting Shannon's approach, picking at his teeth with a quill and a self-satisfied air.

"Lookin' for somethin'?" he grunted, as Shannon dismounted.

"Yeah," Shannon agreed. "I'm looking for Scott Lucas, the foreman here. You must be him, I suppose."

He said it not so much as a question as a statement, holding out his hand. The other eyed it aloofly, making no move to take it.

"No," he denied, "I ain't Lucas. He ain't here any more."

"Not here?" Shannon was taken aback. "Then where is he?"

"Search me." The toothpick waved to a self-satisfied shrug. "I fired him, a spell back. No tellin' where he went to."

"*You* fired him?" Shannon retorted, staggered. "And who the devil gave you the right to do that?"

"Who? Reckon a man's got a right to do as he pleases on his own ranch. I'm Tom Shannon, an' I own this place. What's it to you?"

"I thought something smelled around here," Shannon said bitterly. "Now I know it does. Since it happens that I'm Tom Shannon. I was delayed in gettin' here —"

He stopped, observing that several of the hands, who had been loitering near, were approaching now, with rising interest. It seemed to Shannon also that an attic window, high up in the house, close against the hill, blinked at him for a moment. But that notion was almost as fantastic as some of the things he was hearing. Now the window was blank again.

The man who had proclaimed himself to be Tom Shannon pocketed his toothpick, his eyes narrowing. He drew a cigar from a pocket with cool deliberation, tore off the wrapping, licked down a loose bit of leaf, and stuck it in the corner of his mouth.

"That all you got to say?" he asked with elaborate sarcasm. "You was delayed in gettin' here, hey? Well, you an' me are in agreement on one thing, feller! There's a smell

26

around here — of skunk! Strong, since you rode up! But don't try any cock and bull story. It won't get you anywhere. I'm Tom Shannon. Ask anybody. I inherited this ranch from my uncle, Bart Redding. I been in possession quite a spell. I showed the proper papers, to prove who I was. Everything's in order at the court house. And if this is your idea of a joke, all I've got to say is that it's a damned poor one!"

"A joke!" Shannon choked. Understanding was coming to him. "Why, you infernal thief! It was you who shot me — or hired it done! Then robbed me, takin' my papers, figurin' to steal this ranch! I'm beginnin' to see the whole thing now —"

"That's enough!" The other man's voice crackled angrily. "I don't have to take this sort of thing, and I won't! Like I say, I'm Tom Shannon, this is my ranch, and that's all there is to it! I'm a reasonable man, but damned if I'll put up with any such talk from some imposter who wants to run a sandy! Get out!"

Shannon went cold with anger. Cold with an anger which threatened to choke him. But he controlled it, looking around aware that here was danger, real and grim. Those attacks on his life had not been coincidence, or for mere robbery. The last time he had

27

been robbed and left for dead. And, save that Thad Gormley had happened to discover him and been a doctor of no mean ability, he would be dead enough.

But he saw now that there was more of a plot than he had guessed. Someone had learned of his inheritance of this ranch, had apparently found out that no one in this country had ever set eyes on him. He would arrive, a stranger, friendless and unknown — unless he had those papers to prove his inheritance and identity!

Knowing that he was heading for Vermillion riding alone, this other man had laid his plans accordingly. If he had those papers, he was close enough to Shannon's description, as to height, color of eyes and hair, to pass himself off for a man whom no one knew.

So he had fired that shot, or hired it done, which amounted to the same. Now he was in possession, and while Shannon's sudden appearance had probably startled him, he was sufficient of a gambler not to show it. He intended to remain in control.

Shannon had a hunch that his uncle would have had a decent bunch of men working here. If so, this fellow had gotten rid of them, along with the foreman. Shannon had seen this sort of a crew before.

Capable men, but hard — gun-hawks, hired because of their ability to use a gun, and their complete lack of scruple in doing so. If their employer were to give the word, they would gun him down without hesitation.

Shannon choked down his wrath, aware that he stood on slippery ground. A thin triumph was coming into the imposter's eyes.

"That's one trick that didn't work, feller," he grated. "And now I've got a word of advice — good advice! Get to hell out of here — clear out of this country! You've heard of folks travelin' for their health! Well, that's what I'm meanin'!"

Shannon eyed him levelly.

"Looks like you've got the upper hand, right now," he granted. "So I'll go. But don't make any mistake! This is my ranch — and I'll be back!"

THREE

Shannon rode, with the uncomfortable feeling that at any moment he might get a bullet in his back. Already he had stopped one treacherous shot from this man's gun. But he did not look back until he had gone some distance. When he did, it was not the men who caught his attention.

Something seemed to blink at him again from that attic window. As though someone behind it was trying to signal.

"There's shenanigans goin' on here," Shannon growled to himself. "But the best way's to move with the law behind me." He headed back for Vermillion.

The sign, tacked on the riser of a stairway which led up the outside wall of a saloon to the second floor, indicated the office of Ned Files, lawyer. Shannon liked the brevity and simplicity of it. There were other lawyers in Vermillion, as their signs proclaimed. One of them was a Counselor at Law. A second gloried in being an attorney, while a third was a barrister. Shannon climbed the stairs to Ned Files' office.

He discovered Files at his desk, with his feet upon it, and his chair tipped back against the wall. Gentle snores arose. Files was a lean and lanky man, with a disordered thatch of sandy hair and a slight grin on his face, even in sleep. He awoke, stared, then lowered his feet and bowed, all in one continuing gesture.

"Good afternoon, sir," he said. "I fear I must have dozed. Not too loudly, I hope. My motto, sir, is work when there's work to do. And when a job is done, by all means get a nap if you can. I've been catching up

30

on my sleep since coming to Vermillion," he added with a twinkle. "And now, what can I do for you?"

Shannon liked him. Here was no apology, no false pretence of a lot of work which was patently non-existent. He grinned in return as he deposited his hat on the desk and sat down.

"My name is Shannon," he said. "Tom Shannon. Maybe you've heard it before?"

Files' interest quickened.

"It would be an understatement to deny it," he agreed. "And like a war-horse, I seem to scent battle afar — but not too far."

"You're right," Shannon nodded. "The fellow on Thunder River Ranch who claims to be me is an imposter. Like to hear my story?"

"As your lawyer — I hope — it will be necessary. As one human being with a big bump of curiosity, I shall be delighted. Proceed."

Shannon did so, recounting what had happened during the winter. Files listened with attention, asking one or two questions, and his face grew grave.

"And so he warned you to get out of the country, if you valued your health," he murmured. "Judging by what happened to you in the first place, that was probably no

31

idle threat."

"I figure I'll have a fight on my hands," Shannon agreed, and there was a set to his jaw which impressed the lawyer. "I'll look after that end of it. But the way things seem to be tangled up in the courts, I need your help."

"And you'll have it, right down to the last ditch," Files assured him. "Though I must admit that it doesn't sound too encouraging. Having made the acquaintance of this other Shannon, as he calls himself, and having heard your story, I believe you — all the way. Maybe I'm prejudiced because I know that he's a skunk. But I don't suppose that your story will make much of an impression on the court — not unless we can furnish an array of legal proofs big enough to choke a cow. Our local judge, while a most estimable character, is, between the two of us, stubborn as a balky mule. And it seems that, having robbed you, this other fellow has all the legal proofs.

"In fact, as I remember it, he came here several months ago — without the proofs. But he explained that they were coming by mail, and would arrive shortly. Not so long after that, he did furnish them. At about the time, I'd say offhand, that you were shot."

32

"That's interesting."

"Very. But not what the law calls proof. This lawyer who told you about the ranch, now. What did you say his name is, and the town?"

"A Mr. Sylvester Dwyer, in Poncas."

To his surprise, Files' face fell.

"Dwyer?" he repeated. "That's bad."

"How do you mean?"

"He's dead. I read an account of it some weeks ago. Some sort of an accident. Whether that had anything to do with his having handled your case — and they were making certain that he wouldn't be around to dispute who the right owner was, or if it was a normal accident, your guess is as good as mine. Only this plot to get your ranch seems to be well laid."

Shannon was disturbed.

"That means I've no one to back my story," he said.

"It means, at least, that the man who could prove you were the owner is gone," Files conceded. "The situation resolves itself down to the fact that this bogus Shannon has all the legal proofs. Likewise, he's in possession, with a tough crew to back him up. A crew which he brought in with him, so that they're all loyal to him. Possession is a rather impressive nine points of the law, under the circumstances."

"Sounds so. What do we do next?"

Files glanced at a small alarm clock, ticking noisily on a shelf.

"The hour being what it is in the afternoon, it follows as the tail the cow, that His Honor and Sheriff Pesky — did you ever hear a more appropriate name? — will be engaged at checkers. About game sixty, of the third and decisive round. We will call on them, providing the sheriff is winning. If by some freak of chance Judge Weldon is having a run of luck, we will lurk discreetly in the background until he has won his game and is in an expansive mood. But we will need to fortify ourselves with legal proofs. The thing of first necessity is to produce witnesses who can testify that you are, always have been, and therefore must be, the one and only Tom Shannon."

"I'm afraid that's going to be hard to do," Shannon said. "I've always been fiddle-footed. I've known a lot of folks, but it'd be hard to get hold of any of 'em. And all they could do would be to say that I'd given the name of Shannon."

"Which, while helpful, is scarcely conclusive. You have no old-time buddy, who really knows you?"

"I'm afraid not."

"Let's return to Poncas and Sylvester Dwyer. He had no partner?"

"No. He was all alone."

"No clerk, even, or stenographer?"

"I didn't see any."

"He must have been like me, honest and poor. You did not, by any chance, visit a notary, while with him? Or appear before a judge on some aspect of the business?"

"There was some notary work, but he handled that himself. He was satisfied with my claims, and the papers I'd always had, since I was a kid. They're gone, now. And we didn't see anybody else."

"The luck seems to be with your rival," Files sighed. "I suppose it would be too much that you should have a birth certificate, or the means of obtaining one?"

"I was born in a covered wagon, out on the trail. That's all I know about it."

"Fitting, and in the best of tradition, but scarcely helpful. You have no living relatives who know you? Though I suppose if there had been any, they too would share in the ranch?"

"Guess I'm the only one of the family. I had heard that I had an Uncle Bart, but I'd not seen him since I was a baby."

"My friend," Files said solemnly. "You don't need a lawyer. What you want is a bigger and faster gun than this other man. That's extra-legal advice and unethical, but I think you get what I mean. And even that might not be so good. In addition to a tough crew, the report has it that this man who masquerades in your name is a tough hombre himself, and knows how to use a gun."

"I'm not so bad that way, myself," Shannon nodded.

"That, at least, is encouraging." Files glanced out the window, turned back. "Apparently you have at least disturbed his complacency, by revealing that you are alive. Take a look."

Shannon obeyed. The man who claimed to be owner of Thunder River Ranch was riding down the street, flanked by a couple of his crew.

"Apparently he does not propose to give you any chance to do things while he is not around to counter them," Files added. "As I said, I believe you. But it looks to me like a mighty slim chance to get anywhere, even if you might, by some chance, outfight him. The land is his, legally, until you can prove him an imposter and establish your own identity. And if you stick around and pester, he'll be out to amend the first mistake, and really kill you. Is it worth it?"

"What would you do?" Shannon challenged.

Files grinned.

"I'd be just fool enough to fight," he said. "With the emphasis on the fool." He clapped on his hat. "Let's get over and see how the checker game is coming, and hope for the best. Our impression, I fear, will be an unfortunate one upon His Honour. He has long been soured on life and those who are so unfortunate as to have business before him, and the way our Pesky sheriff has been beating him at checkers has curdled the last drop of the milk of human kindness left in him. And yet Bill Pesky says he needs these games to keep a hold on sanity!" For a moment there was a strange look in the lawyer's eyes. Then he shrugged.

"He will consider, with the bard, that all men are liars, and we the chiefest among them. But it seems a necessary first step, things being as they are, and one points interests me strangely. So lead on, MacDuff — you'll damned soon have enough — of old sourpuss!"

On the street he checked to frown. The other Shannon was just disappearing into the office of a rival lawyer.

"Going to see the Counselor — who has all the work he wants handling affairs for

37

the Dusky Lady. The Lady, my friend, is a gold mine which manages to produce a lot of rich ore out of supposedly thin air. H'm. This has an air of conspiracy."

Reaching the court house, now bathed in the last of the afternoon sun, they climbed to the second floor, and paused where a couple of clerks talked in whispers. Files grinned at them.

"How goes the slaughter, Jed?" he asked.

One clerk, lanky, stooped and graying, shook his head mournfully.

"He gets worse all the time," he sighed. "The game's all over but the last jump, and he's been fumin' about that for the last ten minutes, though he knows there ain't no way out of it. Bill Pesky's got him cornered, five kings to two. I don't know what's come over him."

"The kernel of this present trouble," Files explained. "Is that Jed here, being clerk of the court, feels in honor bound to back the judge with a small bet. And so he keenly feels the cold breath of disaster on the back of his neck. Brace yourself, Tom, and come along."

Files led the way into the big, almost empty court room — empty save for the two elderly men who faced each other across a small table and checkerboard in front of a big window, where the sun shone in warmly. The sheriff, not at all in the tradition, was a roly-poly little man, almost bald, save for a fringe of fluffy white hair around three sides of his head, and a genial, almost cherubic face.

Judge Weldon, by contrast, was big, raw-boned, red-faced, and not at all judicial in appearance. He was plainly in a bad temper. Also, it seemed to Shannon, there was a haunting trouble, perhaps a fear, in the back of his eyes. The judge looked up as they entered, then glared at his companion.

"I'll concede it," he snapped. "Since there's work to do, apparently. I'll concede, Pesky. But next time, watch out!"

"Sure, Bill, sure," the sheriff said soothingly. "You just been havin' a tough run of luck. But you almost had me there, a couple of times. I never run up against another checker player could make me hump like you do."

Slightly mollified, the judge arose. The sheriff, eyeing them benevolently, nodded to Files, then left the room. Judge Weldon barked at them.

"You wanted to see me, Mr. Files?"

"If you please," Files agreed. "There is business here which seems to properly come in your jurisdiction, Judge. Allow me to present my client, Mr. Tom Shannon."

"Tom Shan—" Weldon bit the word off in the middle. "Are you crazy?"

"It's a most interesting story, Judge," Files said with gusto. "Most interesting."

"I doubt it," the judge said sourly. "Come into my chambers in five minutes." He stalked ahead, closing the door solidly behind him. Files grinned.

"They've been playing this series of checker games for going on three years now," he explained. "Usually a game takes two or three days. The judge won the first series of a hundred games, 57 to 43, and was pretty cocky, they say. That was before my time. But the sheriff took the second series, 53 to 47, and now they're playing a third series to decide the championship. So of course it's a touchy subject — especially as the sheriff is about five games ahead at the half-way mark."

He crossed to look down at the board, swung suddenly back.

"Say, how about this doctor that you say pulled you through? I almost overlooked him. His testimony should be of value."

Shannon shook his head.

"He couldn't prove a thing, except that I'd been shot and robbed," he pointed out. "We won't drag him in to it unless his testimony would be just what was needed to clinch it. He doesn't want anyone in this town to even know that he's in the country, and you're to keep what I told you about him under your hat. Gormley saved my life. I won't repay him by dragging him in needlessly."

Files nodded, as the judge opened his door and beckoned. His face was forbidding.

"I may as well warn you in the first place, Mr. Files, that there seems to me to be a fishy smell about this whole business," he intoned. "Don't waste my time, now. I'm a busy man."

FOUR

Files did not seem in the least disconcerted. He helped himself to an easy chair, stretching long legs before him. But his voice was brisk.

"I'll be brief, Judge. Here's the size of it. My client, as I told you, is Tom Shannon. In other words, it is our contention that the man now in possession of the Thunder River Ranch is an imposter."

"An imposter?" A curious expression overspread Weldon's face for a moment, then was smoothed away. "That sounds ridiculous," he said shortly. "And you must realize that you are making a most serious charge."

"Of course I realize it," Files agreed. "So is murder a serious matter. And robbery. Allow me to ask one question — to verify what I have heard from other sources. This man now on Thunder River Ranch came here, last fall, claiming to be Tom Shannon. But he did not have the papers to prove it when he came, did he?"

Again, for a moment, it seemed to Shannon that there was a curious flicker in the eyes of the judge. Then he shrugged.

"All the proper and legal papers were presented to me for my approval," he said shortly.

"Exactly. But this other Shannon — as we might term him — told you at the time of his arrival that they had been missent or something, didn't he? But promised to produce them later? And he did produce them — some ten weeks ago?"

There was an appreciable pause. And something — was it apprehension? — shone for a moment in the back of Weldon's eyes.

"I don't know what you're getting at," he spluttered. "There was some delay in the matter of the papers, yes. A perfectly natural thing, as it happened. But I found them conclusive and in order."

Files nodded, uncrossing his legs.

"Mr. Shannon, here, was on his way to Vermillion, some ten weeks ago. He was shot, robbed of his papers — which you have seen since — and left for dead, on the other side of Thunder River. A man over that way chanced to find him, discovered that he was still alive, and took him to his cabin, where he nursed him back to health. Mr. Shannon came on here today, to discover for the first time that someone else was on his ranch, claiming to be himself."

Judge Weldon pulled thoughtfully at the lobe of his right ear. His face had grown blank as he listened.

"Have you any proof to substantiate these charges?" he asked.

"There's the rub, Judge," Files confessed ruefully. "All of Mr. Shannon's papers were stolen from him. His lawyer, back in Poncas, who could readily have verified everything, has unfortunately died in the interim. And, having been a fiddle-footed cowboy all his life, Tom here has no one who could do any more than say he had given his name as Tom Shannon. Of course, having made that claim at various places, years ago, should have some weight."

The judge tugged harder at his ear.

43

"It might give a little," he admitted gloomily. "But it's still hearsay evidence, of course. Even if this gentleman is Tom Shannon, that is no proof that he is the nephew of Bart Redding. I must say that this story has a far-fetched quality to it, at best. Mr. Shannon — the man now on the ranch — arrived in this country as expected, answering every qualification, and I have found his papers to be in order. He is in possession. And you should realize, Mr. Files that to change things in such a case you must have incontrovertible legal proof of what you charge. Frankly, I'm surprised at your bothering me about this at all."

"I'm doing it for just one reason, Judge," Files explained. "We intend to get that proof, though it may take a while. Meantime, we want you, and everyone else, to know what we claim, and what the situation is."

"And just what do you claim?" Weldon asked bluntly. "That the man in possession of Thunder River Ranch is an imposter?"

"That — and that he did, or caused to be done, attempted murder, and the robbery of the papers which my client had in his possession at the time."

The judge snorted.

"Rubbish!" he scoffed. "I don't believe it.

44

Mr. Shannon is a friend of mine, and he is not that sort of a man." His eyes narrowed, swinging to Shannon. "Who is this man who found you and nursed you back to health, sir? If a man of repute, his testimony might be interesting."

"It might be, and if necessary I can produce him," Shannon agreed. "But unless it becomes so, I'd rather not have to, but just to keep this between the three of us. He used to live in Vermillion. And his memories of it are pretty painful —"

"What's his name?" the judge barked.

"Gormley. Dr. Thad Gormley —"

Shannon stopped, astonished at the change in the judge. He had understood, from what Gormley had told him, that there had been a lot of ill-feeling against him in the town, but he had supposed that most of that would long since have been forgotten. Nor had it occurred to him that a man in the position of Judge Weldon would be much concerned.

But now Weldon was swelling like a strutting turkey gobbler. His face reddened, cheeks puffing out. Then the storm burst.

"Gormley!" he shouted. "That infernal charlatan! That — that murderer! Gormley! And you have the nerve — the unadulterated gall, to come here, to me, with such a

45

tale! To me of all men! Why, you, you — get out! Get out, I say, before I have you locked up for malicious malingering! Get out!"

Files appeared almost as astonished as Shannon at this outburst. But there was nothing to do, or to be said, in the judge's present mood. They retreated, and the door was slammed shut after them. In the outer hall, they encountered the sheriff, looking more cherubic than ever. He nodded cheerfully.

"Sounds like you've stirred him up plenty, this time. Ned," he said. "What's that I thought I heard him shoutin' about Gormley?"

Files led the way into the sheriff's own adjacent office, and closed the door.

"We wanted that kept quiet," he explained. "But why should Gormley's name stir him up so?"

Bill Pesky shook his head, pointing to chairs.

"You ever hear of Gormley before, or know anything about him?" he asked.

"Of course, I've heard of him," Files admitted. "He left town not long before I came here. But I don't put too much stock in loose talk. And the fact remains that he saved Mr. Shannon's life. Let me explain the whole thing to you, Bill. You'd ought to know anyway."

"Be glad to know," the sheriff agreed. "Fire away."

Having a respective listener, Files gave a somewhat more detailed account of the whole affair than he had done with Judge Weldon. Bill Pesky listened, occasionally asking questions, then shook his head.

"You was lucky, feller, to have Gormley find you," he said. "I used to think a lot of Thad. Darn good medico. I always did think so, an' still do. And so he's hangin' out over there, is he, makin' a hermit of himself — and even I didn't know about it! Poor Thad!"

"You believe our story, then?" Files demanded.

The sheriff nodded.

"Reckon so," he conceded. "Taken by an' large, some of it sounds sort of incredible, I'll have to admit. But I knew Bart Redding. Mighty nice feller, Bart was. A white man, as you might say. It's set me wonderin', here for a spell, how Bart could have him a nephew like this feller that's on the ranch now. Just didn't seem possible. Knowin' Bart, I c'n easy credit the whole thing."

Thoughtfully, he delved into a pocket, pulled out a plug of tobacco, worried off a chew, and returned it to his pocket again.

"But my believin' it or not, don't have a danged thing to do with the rest of it — or with legal matters, nor such things as keepin' the peace — within reas'nable limits," he added. "Don't get me wrong. Might have been better if you'd talked to me first, Ned. Mebby I could have made the jedge see it in a sorter more fav'rable light — when he was a winnin' a game, say. Though I'd of had to keep quiet about Thad Gormley, of course."

"But why should the judge have it in for Gormley?" Files wondered. "Some of the crowd — I can understand that. But the judge is an intelligent man! Yet he acted like a madman when Gormley was mentioned. Called him a quack, a charlatan and a murderer! It strikes me, after what Gormley did for Shannon here, that he must be rather above average as a doctor. So why a man like the judge should hate him so —"

"Thad was above average," the sheriff agreed. "Most any way you took him. But he had bad luck — one of those breaks that can ruin a man. You see, a patient died — and folks said the doc poisoned her. That was plumb ridiculous, of course, since she was — well, more or less Doc's sweetheart. But that was one reason people thought he

48

wanted to get rid of her. And it was what hit Thad so hard. He might have been able to stand the rest. But that sure got him."

They were silent, understanding. No wonder it had knocked him out. The sheriff leaned, aimed at a spittoon, and sighed.

"I'll have to ride over and see Thad, one of these days," he declared. "We was good friends. I'm a little s'prised he didn't let me know. But I guess he figgered everybody here had turned against him. Don't much know's I blame him. They tarred an' feathered him, and rode him out o' town on a rail." His teeth clicked angrily. "I was out of the county at the time," he added apologetically.

"Sounds like a rotten deal for the doc," Files agreed. "But what makes the judge so cantankerous? He's a good friend of yours, Bill, and you were a good friend of Gormley's —"

The sheriff spat grimly.

"The girl was Weldon's daughter," he explained. "It made a diff'rent sort of a man of him — nigh drove him crazy. That's why he hates Gormley so bad."

FIVE

Shannon had set out that morning, expecting to be at home on his own ranch by night. Now he was up against the toughest proposition he had ever faced. The money which had been in the bank, any amount of which he might have had when at Poncas, was under his enemy's control.

He'd have to get a job — if he could. Even that might not be easy. The bogus Shannon was coming down the street. Now he increased his pace.

"You still in this country?" he demanded loudly. "Didn't I tell you to get out?"

He was nervous, Shannon saw. Uncertain about the outcome if Shannon made a fight of it. That knowledge was pleasant.

"Listen, feller," Shannon retorted. "Who you are, I don't know — except that you're not Tom Shannon, like you claim, nor owner of Thunder River Ranch. I'm sure about that, since I'm Tom Shannon. And I'm stickin' tight in this country till I prove it, and run you out!"

He had spoken with deliberate loudness in turn, aware that more than one man on the street had turned to listen, observing too, that windows in the court house were filling. The heads of Judge Weldon and

50

Sheriff Pesky appeared at once.

His rival hesitated. Clearly, he was disconcerted that Shannon should face him so boldly. If he wanted trouble, Shannon was ready for it. And under these circumstances, with the law watching, he dared not go too far. He shrugged.

"Sounds like you're askin' for trouble, feller," he said. "Comin' here with such a yarn, tryin' to steal a ranch. It won't do. If you had any case, the law'd back you up. And so I'll repeat what I said before, aimin' it as a friendly warnin'. Better get out of this country and forget it!"

He turned and strode away. But he had given public warning. Shannon had no delusions as to what that meant, and, as he was not long in finding out, neither had anyone else.

The sun was setting, a colder breath blowing across the hills. Shannon approached half a dozen cattlemen, asking for a job. Without exception, though somewhat regretfully in at least a couple of cases, they turned him down. Some said curtly that there was no work, at this time of year. But one grizzled old-timer was more truthful.

"Feller," he said. "I admire yore spunk — and I'd like to take you on. But if Shannon — or whoever he is, seein' as you claim to be Shannon — if he says no, then it's no. He's boss of Thunder River, and everybody knows it. I got all the trouble I can manage, without takin' on no more. Reckon other folks'll feel the same. I'm sorry, but that's how it is."

Shannon held no resentment toward these men. He had a pretty good picture in his mind of what conditions were like in the Thunder River country since the coming of the man who now stood in his rightful place. He had seen such things in other places, and they were not pleasant.

Thunder River was the biggest ranch in this section of country. Possession meant power. The others dared not openly antagonize its boss by hiring or giving sanctuary to a man whom he had warned to get out of the country.

But to make a fight he had to stay here. Thad Gormley would welcome him back, but Shannon had no intention of returning there. It would be poor payment in return for what had been done for him, to bring down upon the medico the still rankling bitterness of this community.

Gormley had wanted him to accept a loan that morning, but he had refused. He didn't have even enough money for a hotel room. Shannon stood, debating a plan which had suddenly come to him, so reckless that it left him even a bit startled. But its very boldness was in its favor. He swung around, then halted as someone came hurrying toward him. A girl of twenty or thereabouts, who looked out of place in levis and Stetson, with spurs on her boots and a gun buckled man-wise about her waist.

She was pretty, too feminine looking, with blue eyes and soft brown hair framing an oval face, too dainty for such equipment. Yet she was undeniably at home in them. And she was, just as certainly, approaching with the intention of speaking to him. Her voice was soft, but direct.

"Mr. Shannon?" she asked.

"Why, yes," Shannon agreed. "That's my name, ma'am."

He observed that heads had turned, and that, just across the street, the other man had just stepped out from a saloon and was watching as well. There was heightened color in the girl's cheeks, as if she too were aware of this audience, but otherwise she gave no sign.

"I'm Nancy Adams," she said. "I own the Arrow Ranch. I understand that you're looking for a job. Well, I want to hire a man. How about it?"

The directness, the unhidden challenge in

her words, in front of the bogus Shannon, startled him and excited his admiration. Here was a job. And behind the offer, he sensed, was more than met the eye. He saw the other man take a sudden quick step, a surge of color coming into his face. Then, as quickly, he checked the impulse and watched.

"If you're sure you want to hire me, ma'am, I'll be glad to get the job," Shannon agreed.

"I'm sure," Nancy assured him. "Have you a horse? If you have, we'd better get started right away."

"Right here," Shannon said, and stopped. Now his enemy was crossing the street. His voice was almost pleasant, but there was warning in it as he addressed himself to Nancy, sweeping off his hat.

"Evenin', Miss Nancy. Excuse my hornin' in this way, but are you sure you want to hire this feller?"

"Perfectly sure," Nancy Adams assured him, and her voice was cold. But the other man smiled.

"There ain't no need for you to worry your head, about a crew — nor nothing," he persisted. "You'd ought to know that, Miss Nancy."

For answer, she turned her back on him.

He colored, and his tone was not quite so pleasant.

"In any case, I don't think I'd hire this feller," he advised. "I don't think you'll find him trustworthy. Somebody that comes to the country, lyin' about his name to start with —"

Nancy swung about, her eyes flashing.

"I wouldn't trust a man who lies about his name!" she agreed. "But I don't consider that *he* is lying! He claims to be Tom Shannon — and I'm sure that he is Tom Shannon! That's one of the reasons why I'm hiring him!"

Shannon's rival stared at her, his face flushing and paling. Her meaning was unmistakable. Fury was in his eyes, intensified as he flicked a sidelong glance at Shannon, who stood watchfully. But his hand was not far above the holstered gun, and something in his poise made the other man hesitate. He turned suddenly, not trusting himself to speak, and strode back to the saloon which he had so lately quitted.

Nancy Adams was breathing faster. But she was smiling too, as she turned to Shannon again.

"And now, if you're ready," she said. "We'll be riding. We want to get home before dark. Cowards and bushwackers might be ready to take advantage of it!"

■ ■ ■ ■

Part II
The Thunder
River Rustlers

■ ■ ■ ■

SIX

Despite her desire for hurry, there was delay. The cook had come in from the Arrow with a team and buckboard, to take back a load of supplies. He had seen no reason why he should not stop in at one of the saloons while the groceries were being put up, and one drink had led to another. Now, with an exclamation of impatience, Nancy declared that he must be found.

Presently, perched not too surely on the seat of the buckboard, the cook set out, Nancy riding her horse alongside the wagon to make sure that he did not fall off or go to sleep. Before she started, she thrust some money at Shannon.

"Go into the store and pay for what he got," she instructed. "I couldn't trust him with the money. You can soon catch up with us outside of town."

Shannon took the money, feeling warmed by her trust in him. He had a hunch that there were other factors behind her hiring him, but she was making it plain that she did believe this story. He paid the bill, found his own horse and set out.

Dusk was falling fast, but objects were still distinct, with the last of the false light spread across the town and hovering above canyons and at the edge of the hills. He would follow, for some distance, the same road that he had taken earlier in the day, toward Thunder River Ranch. The Arrow, it seemed, adjoined it.

Just outside of Vermillion the road branched. Here were two valleys, Thunder River coming down from the west, another running to the east, with a shouldering range of hills set in between like a flat-iron, the point of which reached this far. Here it was one road, with a sharp drop-off to one side, leading down to the river, a considerable distance below. On the other hand the bluff rose sharply.

Not far ahead the bluff ended in a short cross-canyon, and here the road from the east swung through to join the road which came down from the west, making one. Beyond the cut-off the mountains made an ever-increasing barrier between the two valleys.

Up ahead, coming toward the town, were

a couple of heavily laden ore wagons. Shannon gave only a glance at them, for so far as he was concerned, the rival mines and their disputes were no concern of his. But something happened to make him change his mind.

A rifle-shot crashed loud on the silence, coming from the thumb of the rocky hill which reared above the road at this point. Almost as it rang in his ears, Shannon's horse jumped wildly, almost unseating him. Ordinarily it was undisturbed by gun-fire, so he did not need two guesses to know that the bullet had been aimed for him, and had instead raked along the flank of the cayuse.

But there was no chance to look toward where the shot had come from, for now events were on the run. At the side of the road was a drop-off down to a jumbled pile of rocks, a hundred feet below, and just out from them was the cold gray ice of the river, snow-encrusted. The bank rose sheerly on the opposite side of the road. And now the leading ore wagon, with its four-horse team, was thundering toward him, the horses in a sudden wild run.

How badly his own horse was hurt, Shannon had no time to determine. In a swift guess he would have said that it was probably more terrified than injured, since it was cutting up such a ruckus. But there was no time for running. The ore team were swerving wildly while the driver yelled and sawed at the reins, the heavy wagon shuttling outward as the horses came abreast of Shannon, cutting off any chance to turn.

Worse, the wagon was hurtling so close to the edge of the road that there was scant space left on it for his horse and himself. Belatedly, the terrified driver was trying to turn the team back before the wagon went off. But the swing would be too late to widen the gap before it hit Shannon.

He gauged the narrowing space, wondering if his horse could keep its footing, and seeing the swing of the wagon, the rear end slamming around and farther out as the front started to turn back, he knew there would be no room for them. Here was the wagon, and there was outer space and darkness.

There came the shock of the wagon box smashing against his horse, driving it out and off as a ball is hit by the bat. But by then, scrambling wildly, Shannon had a hold on the side of the wagon box and was scrambling desperately for safety.

A moment later he was on top of the load of ore, while the wagon thundered along, now back in the middle of the road. The driver turned to look back, and his face lost its color as he saw Shannon, and the angry glint in his eyes.

"G-golly," he stammered. "W-what happened?"

The team was already slowing to a walk. Shannon's voice was brittle.

"That's what I'd like to know," he grated. "Did you do that on purpose?"

His horse, he knew, was lying crushed and dead on those rocks far below. And but for his luck in that quick jump at the smashing wagon, he would have been with it.

"On p-purpose?" The driver mopped his face with a swipe of his sleeve. "G-golly, what makes you t-think that? Somebody was s-shootin' at me — somebody from the Big C outfit, I reckon. These hosses started to run away —"

He was lying. Shannon knew it now beyond any doubt, though up to then he had been willing to give him the benefit of that doubt. The team had not tried to run away. Their quick slowing was sure proof of that. They had run because the driver had made them run, had swerved wildly outward with the deliberate intent of catching him and shoving him and his horse off to their death.

That bullet from the point up above had been aimed to kill him, too — not the driver of this ore wagon. The uncertain light had caused a miss, but the driver had been primed to take quick action if the rifleman failed.

Why? This was something new and sinister, beyond anything he had suspected before. This man tried to blame the whole thing on to the Big C mine, which meant that this ore belonged to the Dusky Lady Mine. But why should those from the mine be out to kill him?

Nancy Adams was coming up now, having ridden quickly back when she heard the shot and sensed that something was wrong. The wagon was stopping, at the outskirts of town. Shannon swung to the ground, but he paused for a parting word with the driver.

"Mister," he warned. "I'll remember you! And you were a lot closer to being dead than you maybe figured! If there's another time, you'll need a lot of luck! Keep that in mind."

While the driver stared at him with slack jaws and bulging eyes, he moved across to where Nancy waited, her face showing her apprehension.

"What happened?" she asked.

"Plenty," Shannon said. "I'll tell you pretty soon. Can you stop the buckboard so I can ride on it? My horse is dead."

"I told him to wait," she explained, and shivered. "Let's get to it!"

"Suits me," Shannon agreed, and walked beside her horse. The dark was fast deepening, so that there was little danger of another bullet from the heights, but he looked around carefully as they went on. He paused momentarily to look down where his horse had gone off, but one glance was enough to confirm his earlier judgment that the animal could not have survived such a fall. The bank was far too steep to climb down after the saddle, except by daylight.

Neither of them spoke until they reached the waiting buckboard. Nancy instructed the somewhat sobered cook to ride her horse, and climbed to the seat beside Shannon.

"Somebody shot at me," Shannon explained then. "But the driver of that wagon pretended he thought it was fired at him, and whipped up his team. Then he swung the wagon out to crowd me and my horse off the road. I managed to grab the wagon and climb on."

Surprisingly, she neither exclaimed nor plagued him with questions. He went on, putting his thoughts in order.

"There was time enough for that hombre who claims he's me — for him or one of his men — to ride ahead and arrange that little party. Likely he figured it'd be a plumb surprise party, me not lookin' for trouble from those connected with the mine. And that's what has me guessing."

"The mines are both on the far side of the range from the Thunder River Ranch," Nancy agreed. "Though it's not so far straight across. But I didn't know that Shannon — or whoever he is — had any connection with their quarrel."

"Has to be some connection," Shannon argued stubbornly. "Well, we'll find out what's going on. Though as you can see, I may be unhealthy to have around. I seem to attract the lightning."

"When it's already striking all around, that makes no difference," Nancy retorted. Their breath and that of their horses was frosty on the night air, curling up like fog. The glare of sun on snow was gone, but though night was at hand, the white world provided sufficient light that objects again stood out with clarity at great distances. They were still following the road which led to Thunder River Ranch.

"Arrow lies right across the river," Nancy explained, as though reading his thoughts. "Which leaves him for a neighbor, whether I like it or not. And I don't."

"Seems like he'd make an effort to get along with you, you being a woman," Shannon suggested.

Hot color washed into her cheeks.

"That's just the trouble," she said. "He's tried to be nice — or what he figures as being nice, but it's just to get what he wants. From what I've heard he has stolen your ranch, but that doesn't satisfy him. He wants Arrow too, and figures that the easiest way to get it would be by marrying me. He had the nerve to tell me, just the other day, that, being a woman, I couldn't make a go of running it, so I'd better just marry him and he'd look after it! That's all he wants, is more land, more power!"

"It might be that you're doing him an injustice, there," Shannon suggested, more than ever aware of his companion's charm. "I feel the same way about him. But he might think a lot of you."

"If he did, he wouldn't threaten me in the same breath, warning me that I'd be sensible to take the easy way," she retorted. "He hasn't been in this country very long, but it's long enough to be easy to see that he's mad with the lust for power and possessions. He has tried to kill you, and robbed, to get Thunder River Ranch. That shows him for just what he is."

"And you felt sorry for me?" Shannon asked, knowing that she had heard the story, now all over the town.

"Maybe, a little," Nancy agreed. "But that wasn't the reason why I hired you. I know that he's a liar as well as a scoundrel, so that means that you're telling the truth, that you're really Tom Shannon, and that Thunder River Ranch belongs to you. So you have something to fight for. And, since he has vowed that he's going to have my ranch as well, we might as well fight him together!"

That was so eminently sensible that Shannon felt his admiration for this girl growing. She was facing the situation clear-headedly, with no false sense of values.

"How big is Arrow?" he asked.

"It's one of the bigger places, next to Thunder River Ranch," she explained. "Ordinarily, we run a couple of thousand head of cattle." She swung to face him squarely. "But right now, we're up against trouble. Most of my crew quit, yesterday. Some of them went right over to *him*. A couple who didn't want to work for him were frightened so that they quit and left the country. I had thought they would be more loyal to Arrow, if not to me," she added bitterly.

"Old hands?" Shannon asked.

68

"Several of them were. A couple had been on Arrow for a dozen years. You see, my father died, just a little while before the other man, who calls himself by your name, came into the country. Since then, I've been running the ranch the best I could. There would have been no trouble — if he didn't go out of his way to make it."

"How much of a crew have you got left?"

"There's the cook, who's a good hand when he doesn't get to liquor. And two others who stayed when the others quit. There's Mike, who's so old and stove-up that he isn't much use any more, but he's loyal. And Andy Devine, who's just a kid." She colored slightly. "Andy's loyal, too. But I — he think's he's in love with me. As I say, he's just a kid. George is the cook, and his wife, Pansy. She helps him, though she isn't able to do much. Not much of a crew for you to build on."

"Me?" Shannon was startled. "What do you mean?"

"The chips are down," Nancy said decisively. "I have to gamble. So do you. I'm sure that you aim to fight, and that you know how to do it. You have that sort of a look. So I'm gambling on you. I want you to act as foreman. This other Shannon was right when he said that I needed a man. But

69

if I need a Tom Shannon, I'll have the real article, not an imitation! And if you're anything like what your Uncle Bart was, then anybody but this other fellow would have my sympathy!"

"Any particular reason, aside from Arrow joinin' Thunder River, why he's so anxious to get hold of it?" he asked.

"Yes," Nancy conceded. "Most of Arrow is on the west side of the river. But there's a slice of it on the east side, and it's shaped like an arrow, cutting right back into Thunder River Ranch for nearly three miles. The strip is a mile wide at the river, though it runs back to a point. It almost cuts Thunder River Ranch in two. This other — Shannon — said it was like an arrow, right into the heart, and that he couldn't have such a thing."

Shannon nodded. That was understandable.

"In the old days, your uncle and his herds went across Arrow land without question," Nancy went on. "I would have been willing to let him do the same, if he had been decent about it. To get back and forth otherwise means a long, hard trail, back in the mountains. There are canyons and hills, which follow the arrow on both sides, so that there is only one good way to cross it

— an easy gap about a hundred yards wide. With a good crew — if we had it — we could hold that and keep him off, and that worries him, of course."

"You haven't told him that he'd have to keep off?"

Nancy colored again.

"Yes. I lost my temper, when he started making threats. It was a foolish thing to do, when I didn't have the power to back it. And his reply was to take my crew away from me. But if he thinks I'm licked, he'll find out differently!"

Now their trail swung out onto the ice and across the river. The valley was wide at this point, with Thunder River in peaceful thrall beneath the ice. Nancy mentioned it.

"It looks peaceful enough now, doesn't it? But when the warm days come, and the ice breaks up, with the snow in the hills flooding down, it's savage — and treacherous."

Back a mile from the river, on higher ground, were the Arrow buildings. Nancy waved a hand.

"I've seen the river spread clear across the valley, two or three miles wide," she said. "And from the amount of snow this year, it'll be that way again in a few weeks."

The Arrow was a well-kept-up place. Shannon met the crew. All were white-haired, with the exception of Andy, who was gawky but promising. Hay had been put up during the summer, to be fed out during the winter months, and they had managed to keep that attended to. Though, when spring work commenced, they would be helpless alone.

"Any ideas where I'll find a new crew?" Shannon asked, remembering the fear which had gripped nearly everyone in Vermillion. If there were idle men in town, they would not hire on here.

"You might find some at Twin Buttes," Mike suggested. "Ought to, in fact."

"I'll try it," Shannon agreed, and stopped as a knock sounded at the door. All of them had gathered in the big kitchen, warmly lamp-lit. Now apprehension ran across their faces. After a moment, George crossed and opened the door.

The man who entered looked to be a townsman, and he seemed ill at ease, nodding and pulling off his mittens.

"Evenin', Miss Nancy," he greeted. "Evenin', folks. I — nice night for a ride, eh?"

Nancy surveyed him coldly, but with a flicker of apprehension in her eyes.

"I'm surprised to see you riding way out here, at any time, let alone now, Mr. Kinstry," she said. "Especially when you could have spoken to me in town this afternoon."

Kinstry's face reddened, more than the heat of the stove seemed to justify. He coughed.

"Well — fact is, Miss Nancy, I was aimin' to speak to you then, but I guess it sort of slipped my mind —"

"What was it you wanted? Won't you sit down?"

"Er — thanks, but I guess not. Have to be gettin' back." Plainly, Kinstry did not relish the errand upon which he had come. He coughed, then plunged ahead desperately.

"The — the thing is, Miss Nancy," he added. "That loan of yours at the bank — it's due the fifteenth. And — well, money's pretty tight, these days. I — I'm afraid we'll have to have it."

"And last week you told me not to worry about it!" Nancy accused. "And you're supposed to be president of the bank! I never thought you'd come to this, Mr. Kinstry."

Kinstry flushed. Here was proof that control of the bank was in other hands. Since Nancy had defied the other Shannon by hiring Shannon, Kinstry had been forced to ride out and deliver this humiliating message. The shame of it was in his face.

"Fifty thousand dollars," Nancy added.

73

"It's a lot of money. But don't worry. We've got some fat cattle, and we'll sell them and you'll have your money. Which, I know, is just what you don't want!"

SEVEN

"Fortunately, that is the only money which is owed," Nancy explained, the next morning. "It does fall due on the fifteenth, for father borrowed the money to buy more land with, a couple of years ago. I hadn't figured on paying it off now. It means selling all the beef that's any good at a sacrifice, where otherwise we could pay it off next fall and never feel it. But at least we can be in the clear."

Her teeth clicked with a determined snap.

"It's just another move to make as much trouble for us as possible. But we can handle it!"

Shannon liked her spirit. But this made a crew more than ever imperative. True, there would be no tedious job of rounding up the herd. Since there was snow everywhere, and the cattle were fed every day, they did no straying. All that would be necessary would be to get them to market. But that meant a drive down beyond Twin Buttes, which would not be easy, at this season of the year.

74

"I'll ride for Twin Buttes today," Shannon decided. "The sooner we have men to back us, the sooner we can fight back."

It would be an all day ride. There was no sun to glare on the snow, but a haze of clouds indicated approaching storm. Selecting a good horse, he set out.

It was evening when he reached the town. All that he could see was a dark huddle of buildings, pinpointed by little yellow lights. He found a stable for his horse and stopped to give it a rub-down in its stall. As he was turning away, he noticed the brand of the horse occupying the adjoining stall. It wore the mark of Thunder River Ranch.

"When did that horse come in?" he asked casually.

" 'Bout an hour ahead of you," was the reply. "Couple of them rode in." The stable-man grimaced. "Look how they treated their cayuses today! Near rode to death. I don't like hombres that'll mistreat a horse."

Shannon was thoughtful as he stepped out into the night. This might be coincidence, but on the other hand it might not. It was possible that the banker had overheard what he was saying, the evening before, while he paused outside before knocking. And he might have repeated it to the man whom he apparently owned as boss.

There was much which was becoming harder to understand as time went on. What was the connection of this rival Shannon with the Dusky Lady mine, that they too would work for him? Certainly there was a bigger gamble involved, for greater stakes, than he had guessed at first.

In any case, with those other riders here, it would be well to tread warily in this town.

He found a restaurant and got his supper, then headed for the biggest saloon. If there were idle men about, they would congregate in such places, partly for the companionship, but mostly because there was nowhere else to go. He did not intend to ask any questions, and so betray himself. If men were here from Thunder River Ranch, they probably would not expect him this soon, neither would they know where to find him. He'd wait and see what they were up to.

As was to be expected, he drew curious looks from the others when he entered the room. Strangers were few and far between at this season of year. A few men were loitering at the bar, some were playing cards at tables, others were frankly loitering and visiting. Shannon paid for a drink and sipped it slowly, looking them over.

The group at one table were looking for another player. One of them caught his eye, and Shannon slid into the vacant chair.

"You'll have to keep the ante low, if I'm to sit in," he said. "I like a friendly game, but I'm not long on cash."

The man who had caught his eye chuckled.

"You'll fit in with us, then," he said. "If a pot was to go bigger'n four bits, somebody'd have heart failure."

They played for a while, saying little, a friendly atmosphere pervading the place. Then one man yawned and pulled out. A bystander slid into the vacant chair, and the game went on, apparently unchanged.

But Shannon soon sensed a new tempo. This newcomer was different, somehow. The others, too, seemed to sense the changed atmosphere and, like himself, to resent it. Nothing was said, but he could feel the tension. His own luck had been running fairly good, and now the newcomer swept the table with his eyes, then reached and transferred his whole stack of chips to the middle of the board.

"Best I can do, with this picayune limit," he said, " 'less somebody has the guts to raise it to man-size."

The man opposite Shannon surveyed the newcomer with a disapproving light in his gray eyes.

"Feller," he said. "This is just a friendly game, to pass the time. Ef'n you want blood, there's them as has money. This is the wrong table for that."

"Looks to me like you hombres could have money, if you wanted it," was the disparaging retort. "It's to be had, you know. But let 'er ride. I've got my chips in, and I'm callin'."

There was a truculence about him like that of a disturbed grizzly. The gray-haired man surveyed him, shrugged, and sat back.

"This was a friendly game," he reiterated. "Till it gets that way again, I'm out of it!"

The newcomer laughed, boisterously, and eyed the rest, a mingled sneer and challenge in his eyes. The others in turn sat back. That left only Shannon. And he sensed now, in a quick intuitive flash, that this whole play had really been aimed at him. The other man, who was apparently, like himself, a stranger in town, was looking at him, the sneer and challenge more open.

"Do I take the pot by default?" he gibed.

Shannon kept a tight grip on his rising anger. This was not the time to play the other fellow's game.

"You called," he reminded, and laid down his hand. "Match it."

There was a momentary silence, an explosive release of breath. Shannon had four aces. A hand with which he might well have raised the bidding to dizzy heights. As it was, the pot belonged to him, but it was an insignificant one.

But, as he had guessed, that was just a by-play, an excuse. Since he had not taken up the challenge, it was a poor excuse, and nothing, by the wildest stretch of the imagination, to get excited about. However, a poor excuse was better than none. The interloper stared truculently for a moment, and his eyes flickered like heat-lightning. Shannon, watching, tensed.

"You damn cheatin' crook!" the trouble-maker blazed suddenly, and, flinging himself back and sidewise, was going for his gun.

Shannon knew that his hunch had been right. He had not seen this man on Thunder River Ranch the day before, but the fellow had made up his mind. That was proof that he had a confederate somewhere in the room who did know. The pair had been sent down here, without loss of time, not only to make sure that he did not get a crew, but to kill him. If the job of disposal could be done here in a strange town, against an unknown, that would be all to the good.

Certainty that there were two of them was in Shannon as he flung himself back, reach-

79

ing for his own gun. His eyes were sweeping the room, racing to the big mirror some distance in front of him. In it now was revealed, as he had feared, what might be the death of him.

There was a second man, behind him, near another table where men had been playing. And though by no stretch of the imagination could this be called his quarrel, he too was aiming to make sure that there would be no slip-up in this try at murder. Shannon had seen him on the ranch when he called there. This man was wheeling, his gun clearing leather as he turned.

Something like a lump of ice seemed to have thudded out of nowhere into Shannon's stomach. Here were odds which it was impossible to beat. They had him pocketed, whip-sawed, and they were set for a killing, on a business-like basis.

But it wasn't going to be quite so simple and cheap as they had figured. That man behind would get him — Shannon had no doubts there. There was nothing that he could do about it. But this interloper who had started the ruckus wasn't going to get off scot-free as he had counted on. Shannon's gun was already in his hand, faster than either of them. And bucking.

He saw the man who had challenged trying desperately to raise his weapon, saw the muzzle tip instead toward the floor and the man himself following it down, pitching across it. Red was already beginning to stain the floor from a welling spot just above his heart.

There had been one other shot, but he had not fired it. Now there was a sudden, almost echoing silence in the room. It came to Shannon, almost like a shock, that he was still alive and unhurt. Yet the man behind him had fired once.

Shannon swung about. The other man was standing, still clutching his smoking gun in one hand. But both that and his other hand were lifted high now, while another man, one of those who had dropped out of the game as the stakes got too high, stood behind him, holding a gun-muzzle hard against his back.

In sudden release of tension, men began to talk, and chairs scraped back. Everyone was exclaiming at once.

"You dirty polecat," the man who held the gun on the second rider said acidly. "That was as dirty a double-cross as I ever hope to see — but I was watching *you!* I saw you ridin' in to town on what used to be *my* fav'rite cow-hoss, with your spurs drippin' blood!"

"Feller, you sure handled that skunk nice," the gray-eyed man said admiringly to Shannon. "I didn't rightly figure out what he was up to, fast enough. Thought he had just too much likker in him. But we better make it a clean sweep, eh, boys, by stringin' up his partner? Looks to me plain enough that they was workin' together. They must have come here just to kill this gent, and I don't approve none of that sneaky way of doing it!"

There was instant and loud approval from the crowd. The man with his hands in the air went as white as the snow beyond the edge of town. This was not working out as they had planned.

"Wait a minute, boys," Shannon suggested. "Let's get this straight, before we do anything hasty. I'm new here, and I never saw this hombre before, even if he did try to kill me." He indicated the man on the floor. "Who are they?"

The man holding the gun on the prisoner, answered.

"They're from Thunder River Ranch. They both rode in to town on Thunder River horses. We ought to know, since we used to work there ourselves."

Shannon's heart jumped. This group, clustered here together, playing quietly for the fun of it — that meant that they were without jobs, and had to husband their resources until spring opened up new jobs. They were the old Thunder River crew, the men whom his enemy had promptly fired when he took over. Here was better luck than he had dared hope.

"You're Bart Redding's old crew, then?" he said.

The gray-eyed man nodded.

"That's us. We ain't no gun-hawks, like this pair — but we know how to use guns, if we have to," and he nodded at the man who had stopped the second killer so neatly.

"Seems like you was some better than them," Shannon grinned. "And lucky for me. Now I'll tell you who I am. I'm Tom Shannon."

He saw the surprise and bewilderment in their faces, and knew that no word of recent happenings at Vermillion had reached here yet.

"What I mean is, the real Tom Shannon, nephew of Bart Redding. That hombre on Thunder River Ranch who claims to be me, is somebody else. Only trouble is, that I can't prove it, right now. I was ridin' for this country, near three months ago, when somebody shot me from ambush and left me for dead. He robbed me — takin' my papers that showed who I was. Yesterday, when I was well enough to go on, I found this other hombre who claims to be me, on the ranch. He'd got possession by showin' the papers that he took off me. He warned me to get out of the country — or else!" He jerked his thumb. "Looks like this try at killin' me now is explained."

There was silence, while the others digested this, then a chorus of excited comment. They asked questions to get it straight in their minds, and seemed to like the way he answered. One thing was apparent. Aside from the pair sent here to kill him, there was no hostility to him, here in Twin Buttes. Everyone, having witnessed the attempt at murder, now believed his story without question.

"Shannon," the gray-eyed man said, holding out his hand, "I'm Slim Moffet, and I worked on Thunder River Ranch for seven years. We're here — all of your uncle's old crew. And out of a job. It sure sounds like you've been handed a dirty deal. But we're right behind you, to go back up there and clean up on that skunk and take the ranch back!"

Shannon's eyes kindled. There was an eagerly assenting chorus from the others. It was the sort of program which appealed to them.

"You're not out a job any longer," he assured them. "I came down here, to find a crew, but this is better luck than I'd hoped for. Right now, you're hired on as crew for the Arrow — which this bird is tryin' to grab as well. As to the rest of the program you mentioned, that'll come."

By this time, as he had hoped when creating a delay, there was an intervention. Bill Pesky had a deputy, stationed in Twin Buttes, and someone had gotten word to him of the impending lynching. Now he arrived and took charge of the prisoner. The fellow deserved hanging, but Shannon preferred for the law to handle such a case. There was some grumbling as the gunman was turned over, but they followed Shannon's lead without question.

There were ten men in this old crew. Tophands, as was easy to see. Good men, and loyal, with a grudge of their own to settle as well. The discovery that they had not only been turned out of their jobs as winter was setting in, which was against the code of the rangeland, but that they had been dispossessed by an imposter, made it a personal matter with them.

Even so, he would not have a crew of more than half the size that his rival had surrounded himself with. But it was a crew that he could depend on.

His trip here had turned out much better than he had hoped for. These men were well-known and respected in Vermillion, and the story that they would have to tell, of how a pair from the new crew on Thunder River Ranch had come down here to try and murder him, would have an effect on public opinion. It was a story which could lose nothing in the telling.

They were early on the road, the next day. The storm still held off, though the clouds were thicker, lower, blotting away the hills. They rode in a gray world, but in a spirit of good-fellowship. Shannon liked these boys, every one of them, and he knew that they liked him as well. And if trouble came, they were ready for it. Unwittingly enough, the bogus Shannon had considerably strengthened Nancy's hand, in getting rid of a timorous and unsatisfactory crew, and also arranging it so that it was being replaced by a bunch like this.

By noon it commenced to snow, and the storm gradually thickened as they rode. There were two roads — the little-used one which he had followed down the west side of Thunder River until it made a junction with the main one, or this regular road, leading across the river to Vermillion. He chose the main one today. It would do no harm to appear in Vermillion with the old crew of Thunder River Ranch behind him. The thing would shock his rival, and furnish a lively topic of conversation for the rest of the community.

There were three inches of new, fluffy snow on the old when they came to town at mid-afternoon, and it was coming down so thickly by then that it was impossible to see far in any direction. Slim Moffet opined that it would keep on storming all night, and probably the next day as well.

"We always get one big snow to sort of wind up with, about this time of the year," he said. "After that, we'll have a little kind of settled spell. Then, all at once, it'll start to come spring — and when she comes in this part o' the country, she comes fast. Just kind of busts loose. And when you see the break-up in Thunder River, you'll know what I mean."

Shannon could guess. When that happened, Arrow would be isolated from Thunder River Ranch and the part of Arrow on the east bank, and from Vermillion itself, for a period of weeks. While the water ran at flood-tide, nothing could cross the river, save by boat, and that would be risky business. During that time, such trading as was necessary was done at Twin Buttes. Though, forewarned each year, a good supply of all necessary articles was laid in, so that few trips to the distant town were necessary.

All of that, however, was in the future. Winter was in full control now, and showed no signs of relaxing its grip. Two or three people were on the streets of Vermillion, looking like dim-seen ghosts in the storm. Somewhere behind them, Shannon heard sounds, and interpreted them rightly to mean that the stage was arriving, having followed the same road as themselves. Though this came with a jingle of sleigh-bells, and on runners.

Someone recognized the men who rode with him, stared, waved a hand in greeting, and hurried toward a saloon to spread the news. Then the stage came in sight.

Pulling up, across the street, Shannon watched as it came up and stopped. Ordinarily its arrival was an event, but not many were braving the weather to meet it today. Then he recognized one of the few who seemed interested. A muffled, heavy-coated figure was coming down the street, hurrying a little as though his arrival was belated. Judge Weldon.

The door of the stage opened, and a couple of men climbed out and, after a quick look about, hurried off. No one paid any attention to them. Then a third passenger stepped out, pausing a little uncertainly. Shannon took another involuntary look at sight of her.

She was a girl, not over eighteen or nineteen, tall and slender. She appeared both wistful and frightened, manifestly uncertain. Under her hat shone hair like fine spun gold, and a rarely sweet face. She turned, and saw the judge approaching, and for a moment she turned to stone.

Judge Weldon had seen her at the same moment. He stopped in his tracks, and for a moment his face was a twisted study in emotions — incredulity, unbelief, joy. With a choking cry, he took an unsteady step forward, holding out his arms to her.

"Louise!" he gasped. "Louise!"

EIGHT

Slim Moffet, sitting his horse beside Shannon, was also staring as though beholding a ghost. Shannon heard his gasp, and turned his head for an instant to look, then swung back. For here was a strange and, he sensed, somehow terrible drama.

The girl did not appear to hear the strangled cry of the judge or even to see him. She had turned and was walking, moving like a sleep-walker, in the opposite direction. Now they saw that a carriage waited, with a team of black horses and side and front storm curtains enclosing it below the raised top. Reaching this, someone assisted her quickly inside, then the carriage was gone in the storm.

Judge Weldon had started to run. He stopped, panting, and the twisted, tortured look on his face caught at Shannon's sympathies. Turning, the judge moved off, walking now like a man whose age has suddenly caught up with him.

Beside him, Slim Moffet swore again.

"He thinks he's seein' a ghost," he said. "And damned if I don't think he's right!"

"What do you mean?" Shannon demanded.

Slim turned to look at him, and while it might have been the illusion of the storm, Shannon thought that his face was pale.

"He thought that girl was his daughter," Slim explained. "Though she's been dead the better part of a year. But I sure can't blame him for that. She sure looked like her."

"Then you don't know who she was?"

"Who? Me?" Slim's grin was lop-sided. "I ain't acquainted with many ladies, so far as that goes. I'd of made the same guess the judge did — even knowin' I had to be wrong. Reckon she's somebody come for a visit somewhere, seein' how she arrived. Bet that gave him a bad turn, though."

"Did you recognize the carriage?"

"Never saw that outfit before. This has plumb got me guessin'. Seems like she'd of kind of stopped to be polite, when she saw him speakin' to her. Anybody could see he was an old duffer, and not a masher."

On sudden impulse, Shannon rode ahead. The tracks of the buggy wheels could be seen in the snow, but beyond were more wheel and sleigh marks where wagons came down from the mines, and all sign was lost in the steadily falling storm.

Here was something strange. And considering this tragedy which had come into the judge's life, Shannon could understand how the man had become soured. But there must be some good in him. The sheriff stood by him, remaining his steadfast friend. And everyone vouched for Bill Pesky.

"Him and the judge are both named Bill," Slim volunteered, after someone had mentioned the subject. "Used to call them the two bad Bills, around here. They didn't mind. Folks don't do it no more, though. They sort of figure the judge as bein' the bad one. Kind of feel sorry for Pesky, I guess. He's about the only man who used to be friendly with the judge that still sticks to him, same as ever. And I reckon the judge ain't pleasant company, even for him."

Outside of town, where the road divided, Shannon scrutinized it closely. He had had a vague and undefined hunch that the fresh marks of carriage wheels might be found, heading up the road they were taking — toward Thunder River Ranch. But there were no such signs to be found.

The storm continued as heavy as ever, and the early dark was upon the land when they reached Arrow. Shelter and warmth was welcome, and Nancy was jubilant at Shannon's success.

"This is better than I'd dared hope for," she said, welcoming the new hands. "I supposed that you boys had left the country a long time ago."

Slim grinned slowly.

"We sort of set out to shake the dust of it from our boots," he conceded. "But by the time we'd got to Twin Buttes, seemed like we'd gone far enough. And this country is sort of like home. Also, Junior here, he had a hunch that something'd turn up if we stuck around a spell."

Junior grinned bashfully. He was a man of

92

thirty or so, slow of movement, tipping the scales at nearly three hundred, so that it required a good horse to carry him. But, though he said little, he seemed to be a favorite with the rest of the crew.

"Well, I was right, wasn't I?" he asked, and let it go at that.

The wind was a banshee wail outside as Shannon went to sleep. It was still blowing the next morning, though the snow had stopped falling. But there was an additional fifteen inches of it since the storm had started, and the wind had played wild games with it. In some places the ground was swept bare, in others huge drifts were piled. If this was winter's last great effort, it had been at pains to show what it could do.

It was Mike who brought the news, as the rest of them were at breakfast. He burst into the room, red-faced from haste.

"The herd!" he gasped. "They're gone!"

"Gone?" Nancy protested. "They can't be. They wouldn't go away from their feeding grounds, not far."

"That's the way I figgered," Mike agreed. "But I rode for near a mile, lookin', and there ain't a hide ner hair ner track to be seen. They're gone, I tell you."

"Prob'ly drifted with the storm," Andy Devine opined with the brash assurance of youth. "We'll find 'em down river in the brush."

Shannon made no answer to that. He was already slipping into his heavy coat, and he hoped that Andy might be right. But somehow he doubted it. There was something funny here, something strange and sinister.

An ordinary range herd would drift with a storm, that was true enough. But, as Nancy had pointed out, this was no ordinary range herd. These cattle were accustomed to being fed daily, in sheltered coulees and along ice-covered creek beds, where the brush-lined banks gave excellent shelter from even such a storm as this had been. Under such circumstances, they would not drift, but remain stubbornly where they could expect to be fed again.

Yet, as Mike had reported, they were gone. There was a momentary flurry of optimism when Andy reported having found them. But what he had found turned out to be only a handful of cows and young stock, off by themselves, less than a score in all.

Off a couple of miles, where most of the younger stock and cows had been kept by themselves during the winter, fed separately so that they could do better with less competition, everything was as it should be. This bunch was undisturbed, calmly waiting for breakfast to be served. But here too, there was no sign of the missing beef herd.

Junior, astride a cayuse of almost draft horse proportions, shook his head.

"Strikes me they wouldn't drift that way o' their own accord," he said. "Looks like they'd been driven."

Shannon had reached the same conclusion. He was berating himself for not having anticipated such a move and been on guard against it. Still, it was hard to see what he could have done to forestall such a move. It had probably happened the day before, under cover of the storm, long before he had returned with the new crew.

But it all fitted with the pattern of increasing violence and disregard for law which his enemy was showing. They had told Kinstry, the banker, that his money would be paid, even though it meant selling the beef herd now, at a sacrifice. It was apparent that Kinstry obeyed a master's voice, and the man who posed as Tom Shannon was the boss. Kinstry had reported that Shannon was going to Twin Buttes, and another try at murder had been made.

So it was logical that the banker would have reported how the loan was to be paid. Naturally, they did not want the deadline to be met. Arrow was far preferable to the money. Knowing that Shannon was away, and that the few men on Arrow, having thrown out a little hay in the morning, would keep indoors the rest of the day, it had been easy to drive off the herd. For a man who had no qualms about either murder or stealing a ranch, the rustling of a herd was nothing to boggle at.

This was intended as a crippling blow, one which would force Arrow to capitulate. If Kinstry called in the loan, no out-of-country banker would make a new one. Having stolen the herd, with the storm and wind to wipe out all sign, they would aim to see that it was not recovered, at least until after the deadline. Once the ranch was lost, the herd might be found, as though they had only strayed.

"It's up to us to get them back — and in time," Shannon said grimly. He had outlined his belief in a few blunt words, and the nodding of heads confirmed that the others believed as he did. "Chances are they've been gone about twenty hours. They'd of had to stop when it got dark, to rest, and because you couldn't move a herd in such weather after dark anyway. That means that we ought to be able to pick up the trail in not more than fifteen miles from here."

He gestured significantly.

"I'm new in this country. You boys are old-timers, and know it. Now it's up to you to find them. My guess is that they won't be on Thunder River land, since that's the logical place to look for them, if they were rustled by a Thunder River crew. But I may be wrong."

Slim Moffet nodded.

"Looks to me like you sized it up right," he agreed. "But findin' them ain't going to be easy. There's more coulees an' valleys up back than there's fleas on a dog. And with this wind blowin', coverin' tracks —" he shrugged. "But we can do our damnedest."

"We'll divide in three parties," Shannon decided. "One to go down river, then swing west. One bunch to head west. The others up river. But every man in each bunch be sure to keep in gun sound of each other, all the time."

They nodded, understanding the significance of that. All three searching parties, unless they found sign first, were to gradually converge toward the wild rugged hills of the up-river country, where there was room to hide a hundred big herds.

It was a guessing game, as Shannon realized only too well. The storm and the covering wind gave the rustlers a big advantage, but that could be lost unless they were smart. For a big herd would leave fresh tracks in snow as soon as the wind died.

That meant that whoever was clever enough to out-think the others would win. For that reason, Shannon doubted if the rustlers would make any effort to drive the stolen herd out of the country and to market. That would be too hazardous from every standpoint, and it was unnecessary for the accomplishment of his rival's purpose.

So it would be a game of hiding them, in some deep canyon or pocket of the hills. For a few days they would fare scantily, but spring was not far off, and the thaws would remove the snow before they would starve. But now they had to be found.

It was a mean job. Shannon chose to go with Slim and a couple of the others, heading up-river on the west bank, since that seemed most logical to him. Up this way would be the hardest country in which to find a herd. Mike and a crew went south, while Junior led others west.

The wind continued to blow during most of the day, kicking up the loose snow so that at times one could see little farther than had been possible the day before. They found no trail, but even a big herd would have left a scant mark under these conditions. Their horses wallowed through deep snow, frequently forced to turn aside for drifts or canyons. Progress was slow. As Slim had said, this up-river country was a maze, and to explore every possible hiding-place would take weeks or months.

Shannon was interested in the country, particularly across the river. The ranch buildings on the Thunder River Ranch were set near the lower boundaries, and the Arrow land which split the big outfit in two was some miles farther up-river. From across here, Shannon could see the mountains which made that so imposing a barrier.

They found nothing, that day. When night came on they camped, bone-weary, but Shannon had foreseen this and had left orders for Andy to meet them with grub and blankets. George had come also, on his own initiative, and had a hot supper waiting at the rendezvous. When away from liquor, George was a stellar cook.

"Sho," he protested, expertly dishing out steaming hot biscuits and sizzling steaks. "Men that work gotta eat. And besides, this gives me a chance t' show what I c'n do. Back home, Pansy, she makes out that I'm only a good helper. But I used to travel with a chuck wagon and dish up grub with the best o' them. Guess mebby I ain't forgot all I knew."

"If you have, I'd sure like to know's much as you've forgot," one of the cowboys assured him, from around a succulent mouthful, washing it down with black coffee. "Best grub I've tasted in years."

Shannon was glad of the chance to rest. He had worked around for several days before leaving Gormley's cabin, to toughen himself up, but the illness had taken a lot out of him. This work tired him now. But with the morning he felt as good as usual.

The wind had died, the next morning. Any trails made would remain, and the sun shone from a clear sky. The crew which had gone down-river had circled, reporting no sign in a wide radius, which was as Shannon had expected. But, though that gave more men to comb this north country, the job was increasingly hard.

Hope blossomed at mid-day, when they came upon a lot of fairly fresh tracks, a trail made by hundreds of cattle. They followed them, and came upon the bunch late in the afternoon. Hopes plummeted. For this was a beef herd, but they wore the Thunder River brand.

"Dog-gone," Slim Moffet swore dejectedly. "But I thought we had somethin'. It's a'most like they'd done it a-purpose."

Shannon eyed him reflectively.

"Maybe you've got something there, Slim," he said. "Did you happen to notice, back a while, that there had been horses drivin' this bunch? Only those signs petered out a way back."

Slim straightened.

"You mean, this herd was driven in here to cover up another trail — and to lead us astray?"

"What do you think?"

"Sounds likely. No other reason for them bein' in here — or for bein' on the move to start with, either. If we back-track and look sharp, I got a hunch we'll find somethin' we wasn't supposed to see."

"That's the way I figure it, too," Shannon agreed, then regretfully ordered that camp be made. It would be night too soon to back-track and find such a trace as they were after.

But those signs should still be there in the morning, and if they were — well, it was something to go on. There would be no fresh storm overnight.

"We'll be gettin' a break in the weather, some day right soon," Slim opined, as he pulled his boots off. "I feel it in my bones,

Spring ain't far off. She's achin' to bust loose."

"The fifteenth ain't far off, either," Shannon reminded him glumly. "We'd better find that herd tomorrow — or it'll be too late to get them to market ahead of the deadline."

NINE

Impatience stirred in Shannon. He was getting toughened to this work again, no longer tired from a hard day's work. The rest of the crew seemed fagged out tonight, and all of them were already rolled in their blankets and making the air melodious with a chorus of strangely assorted snores. But he was in no mood for sleep yet awhile.

Saddling a fresh horse, he rode downstream, then swung off across the ice-coated river. This was a long chance, but it would do no harm to have a look on Thunder River Ranch itself. Also, there were several things aside from the missing herd which he was curious about.

He came to the strip of Arrow land, thrusting across Thunder River Ranch, hemmed in by the east-west barrier of hills, until it blunted the point of the arrow up against the sheer and almost impassable mountains which ran north from Vermillion. His enemy had been right in his description of the potentialities of this strip of land. It was like an arrow, aimed straight at the heart of the big ranch.

The road through the hills was easy but narrow, and a few hostile gunmen posted on the heights at either side could easily bottle it up.

But there were no marks in the deep snow to indicate that any considerable number of cattle had passed this way for many weeks.

Now he was across the strip and again on Thunder River range. This was land which belonged to him — if he was able to take it! Always he had dreamed of his own, never daring to really hope for anything like this. The news that an uncle had left him such an inheritance had come as a complete surprise. Even then, he had hardly believed his luck. It had been too easy. Experience had taught him that worth-while things had to be earned.

Well, if he regained it, against the prevailing odds, he would have worked for it. When he regained it, he corrected himself. He was going to have his own!

He swung now as far to the east as it was convenient to travel, working close up to the ridge which rose so abruptly and inhospitably to mark the eastern boundary of the ranch. There was a vast slice of land laid out between these hills and the river, ranging from a mile in width to three times that. Mostly it was level or rolling, clear up to the mountain barrier.

He was riding, absorbed in thought, when, to his complete amazement, a voice challenged sudden and sharp.

"Halt! Who goes there?"

With it, came the ominous click of a gunhammer being eared back.

Shannon saw the shadowy figure of a man, not far away. Instantly he realized that here was a watchman, posted here for that express purpose. Incredible as it seemed, this wild section of the range was being guarded. But why?

Even as he saw the sentry, whom he would have missed but for the challenge, he got an inkling of what he was there for. Beyond him was a canyon, twisting back darkly into the towering hills. From this particular spot, with his attention attracted, it was possible to see it. But save for that he would have ridden past without a suspicion that there was such a canyon here. Just a few feet back up it, to help draw his eyes, was the reflected gleam of a camp fire. The blaze itself was out of sight around a bend. Evidently the guard had built it to warm himself.

There was brush and the cover of broken ground conveniently at hand. Shannon risked a shot in the uncertain light to arguing the question. He swung his horse quickly, his first thought being that the stolen herd was being held back in there. But there was no shot, no yelling or pursuit as he pulled back. Though he had no doubt that the guard would now be doubly wary.

Swinging well away, Shannon's curiosity was itching, He had to have a better look. Presently he left his horse tied in the bottom of a coulee, well hidden among a clump of trees and brush. Then, moving on foot, he climbed, circling to keep away from where the sentry could get a look or be apt to hear him.

He was not too much concerned about that. The fellow must be a tenderfoot, and over-zealous. He had betrayed his position at the wrong time, then had done nothing to follow up. The whole thing was puzzling. If the cattle were being held back in there, it was logical that a cowboy would be on watch. But those words, old and stereotyped, had not sounded like a cowboy. Quite the contrary.

And the snow, all around here, contradicted the notion that any cattle had been driven so that they could get into that hidden canyon. Under the fresh fall it was crusted, but unbroken by any hoofs.

He climbed laboriously up the slope, intent on getting high enough to be able to see. Here at the very start of this ridge of hills it was easy to understand why the mountains were such a barrier. It was all that he could do to climb on foot, and the higher a man progressed, from one successive ridge to another, the going would get worse. These hills effectively shut away the valley of Thunder River from the mining operations on the far side.

Or did they? He had finally attained the point which had been his original objective, an excellent spot for an eagle. He had figured that from it he could see down into that hidden canyon, and his guess had been correct. He could see the camp fire, a quarter of a mile away in straight distance, but so close below that he could have heaved a rock and come close to hitting it. The guard himself was out of sight in the shadows.

The astonishing thing was the canyon itself. His brief glimpse of it from below had not disclosed much, but from up here it was staggering. It seemed, in fact, to be two canyons, both leading back into the mountains — perhaps through them to the other side of the valley. Or it could be called one horseshoe canyon, a curved V with its point here, leading back in two directions.

There seemed little doubt that both prongs must go a long way back into the hills. And now, as his eyes became accustomed to the gloom of the canyon bottom, aided at one spot by the firelight, and at another in the opposite branch of the V by a patch of moonlight, Shannon's excitement increased.

The canyon bottom had the look of a much-used road. A road over which heavy wagon traffic moved.

Nothing stirred there tonight. But the snow was trampled flat and hard, and the use of it had certainly been recent. Here was something intriguing. For these wagons had not appeared out on the open land at all. They had gone down one branch of the canyon and up the other — coming and going in the depths of these supposedly impenetrable hills.

This would require more looking into, but there was no time for that tonight. Shannon climbed down again, back to his horse, and rode off in a circle which would bring him within sight of the ranch buildings of the Thunder River, but this time from an opposite direction from where he had seen them before.

They lay there, dark under the moon, no light showing. Or was there one? Something flickered like a candle, high up. A light in that same attic window where he had had the illusion that something winked at him before.

It was gone now, however. Pondering deeply, Shannon headed back across the river and up to his own camp. It was well past midnight when he reached it, but he had a feeling that the time had been well spent.

Of one thing he was certain. The stolen herd was not back in that canyon. His circling had proved that. And if not them, what was it of such a secret and important nature that a guard was kept posted to warn any chance rider away? He had a hunch on that, too, but his guess seemed so far-fetched that he hesitated to give it credence.

They set out the next day with high hopes, which Shannon's discovery of the night had enhanced. But it was, in a general way, only a repetition of the two which had preceded it. Despite their back-track of the other herd and a careful search, there was nothing to be found — only unbroken snow beyond. The other herd had been trailed there to confuse them, and that ruse had worked.

"What do you fellows know about that horseshoe canyon over on the eastern border of Thunder River Ranch?" Shannon asked casually, after they had been riding a while.

The replies were both enlightening and surprising — chiefly on account of the contradictory information they contained.

"It's quite a canyon, that horseshoe," Slim nodded. "Only the danged thing don't go nowhere. Almost comes out on this side of the range, but makes a turn back just before bustin' loose — so that anybody could ride by it an' never guess it was there, if he didn't go right up an' stumble on it, or in it."

That jibed with Shannon's experience. Had the guard kept quiet, he might easily have missed it the night before.

"It's the same way, at both ends," Slim added. "That V kind of spraddles out so the points are better'n two miles apart, north an' south. Both branches run back quite a way. You'd think at least one of 'em would lead somewhere — through to the other side. But they don't. Just end up in blind canyons, deep in the hills. That's all there is to them. Sa-ay — that would be a good place to hold a herd. You don't think."

"I had some ideas, but they didn't drive them in there," Shannon said easily.

With that pronouncement on the oddities of the canyon, Slim seemed to feel that all had been said. His view, of course, would be shared by practically everyone who knew anything about Thunder River Ranch or the canyon. But Shannon figured that he could give the crew a big surprise by telling what he had discovered.

If the canyon was only a blind one, going nowhere, why were a lot of wagons running through it in secret? Why have a guard posted to keep people away? Shannon said nothing, but his far-fetched hunch of the night seemed now a possibility which would be worth investigation as soon as he could find time.

First, however, he had to worry about that deadline and mortgage against the Arrow. Nancy had given him a job when others were turning against him. She had sided with him, making his fight her own. So her fight was also his, and in any case both struggles seemed to be tied up in the one package and equally vital. Some of the strings seemed to be fitting into place.

Leaving a few men to continue the search, Shannon returned to the ranch with the others. He was more troubled than he cared to admit. They would have to report to Kinstry that the herd was lost. But it was more than ever unlikely that the information would move him.

"You've done the best you could," Nancy said loyally, when he reported. "I know that country up north. The herd might be up there somewhere, and we could still hunt for a month and fail to find it, unless we were lucky. And we've still got a few days left."

"And a few tricks up our sleeve," Shannon agreed, but he managed to put more hope into his voice than was in his heart. He and Nancy rode for town, and now there were occasional spots where the wind had swept the snow away, and the sun fell warmly, where it was starting to thaw.

"We'll not be crossing on the ice much longer," Nancy said prophetically, as they rode across Thunder River. "When things start to move around here, they go fast. A few more days, maybe weeks — but I don't think it will be that long."

There were a few cayuses at hitching posts, with the Thunder River brand on their hips. But their riders, for the moment at least, were out of sight. They entered the bank, and Kinstry received them pleasantly.

"I've heard the news," he said. "That your beef-herd has strayed. That's just too downright bad — special comin' at such a time."

"I've heard it said that you used to be a cattleman, Kinstry," Shannon returned. "And so you know well enough that they wouldn't stray far, not of their own accord. And not under such conditions."

Kinstry placed the tips of his thick, blunt fingers together, one at a time, as if, by watching them, he could have a good excuse for not meeting the eyes of either Shannon or Nancy.

"Maybe," he agreed. "Maybe not. The fact remains that they're gone. That is unfortunate."

"Well get them back," Shannon persisted. "How about extendin' the dead-line on that loan a bit?"

Kinstry shook his head. His regret seemed almost genuine.

"I'm mighty sorry," he said. "I wish I could do it. But — well, with that loss, it makes the situation worse, as you can see. I can't do it."

Shannon stood up. There was a biting contempt in his words which brought a quick flush to Kinstry's pale cheek.

"I'd almost feel sorry for you, Kinstry, caught like you are, and not darin' to call your soul your own — yeah, I'd almost feel sorry for you, if you didn't try to curry favor by waggin' your tail as well. As it is, I can't even feel sorry for you."

For a moment, stung, Kinstry did meet his eyes, passing a tongue across dry lips. He tried to make some retort, and could not find the words. They left him so, and went out to the street again. Nancy shivered, as if the interview had been worse than the refusal.

"Well, that was what we expected," she said, matter-of-factly. "What do we do now?"

"I think I'll look in on Ned Files," Shannon decided. "He might have some ideas, or even some news. He said he'd do his best, and I reckon he meant it."

"I'll be down at the Mercantile when you're ready," Nancy said, and turned toward it. Shannon was heading for the lawyer's office when he heard himself hailed.

He swung, to see a man in a business suit, save for chaps and spurs, advancing with outstretched hand. There was a familiar look to him, and then Shannon remembered that he had seen him that evening in the saloon at Twin Buttes.

"How are you, Shannon?" the other man greeted, shaking hands warmly. "Likely you don't remember me, but I saw you the other evenin'. My name's McCreedy, Mart McCreedy. I don't often come up here, but I was hopin' to see you. In fact," he added with a grin, "I was hopin' you'd have managed it to get your ranch back, so that maybe we could do business. I'd like to buy a good bunch of Thunder River beef."

"I sure wish I could accommodate you, Mart," Shannon agreed. "Right now, I'm foreman for Arrow, and I'd have a bunch for you if things had worked out right."

"That so? What went wrong?"

Shannon explained, and McCreedy listened sympathetically.

"That's a shame," he exclaimed. "And Arrow is good beef, too. Though there's none in this country to quite compare with the Thunder River herds. Your Uncle Bart really built up his bunch."

"A lot of people around here still aren't willing to admit that I'm a nephew of his," Shannon said, and McCreedy snorted.

"I know all about it," he declared. "A set of fools! But it's different in Twin Buttes. Everybody there is behind you, hopin' you win out, Any time you need a friend, Shannon — any time you have some beef for sale, call on me. Even if it's a disappearin' sort of herd." He smiled. "I have cash on the barrel-head, top prices, and you can ask any man about Mart McCreedy. In turn, all I've got to say for any of the misguided up

114

this way is that your word is good enough for me, same as your uncle's was."

TEN

Such a forthright statement of confidence and friendship was heartening, though it solved no problems. Encouraged, Shannon went on, to find Files in his office, this time busily writing letters. He looked up to grin.

"Sit down," he invited. "No, not there — here's an old newspaper. Spread it over that chair first. I guess my landlady hasn't dusted lately. Shannon, you see me the picture of industry — writing more letters, in the hope of locating someone who knew you when, as, and if. A slender reed upon which to lean, I grant you, but better than the wind."

"You haven't found out anything hopeful?"

"There's been no time, really. I've written to the names you suggested, but it will take time to get replies. And you weren't too hopeful about them at best."

"No. Chances are that most of them will have moved on, same as I had, long since," Shannon conceded. "Right now, I've the little matter of raisin' fifty thousand dollars on my mind."

"Chicken-feed," Files said airily. "I'll be

glad to loan it to you." Then he grew serious. "I've heard all about that, too — and how the Arrow herd was rustled. No sign of it?"

"Not even a track."

"They tell me that Kinstry used to be a square sort. Seems like he's got himself in bad, somewhere. It's a cinch that he isn't a free agent." He drummed on his teeth with the tip of a pencil, stepped to the window and looked out. Down below, on the street, Judge Weldon was passing. He walked like an old man. It seemed to Shannon as though he had aged years since he had seen him before.

Apparently the same notion was in the mind of the lawyer. He clucked sympathetically.

"The old boy gave us the brush-off the other day," he said. "But I feel sorry for him. It's a sure thing he's half sick, mentally. Thinkin' about his daughter. There's a story around that he thought for a moment that he saw her, here in town the other day, in the storm."

"He did," Shannon said quietly. "Or somebody who looked enough like her that he was fooled."

Files stared incredulously.

"I've heard that," he conceded. "But most

folk don't believe it. Lately here the judge has gone in for spiritualism, or something like that — messages from the dead, all sorts of crazy things. Folks figure that was some more of it."

"I was there," Shannon explained, and told what he had seen. Files whistled.

"No wonder he looks beat out the last few days," he nodded. "Must have given him a bad turn. But where did she go to? I never heard of such a woman anywhere in this country."

Shannon shrugged. He was remembering his first suspicions, and how he had been able to obtain no evidence to back them up. He still looked out without much interest, now that Judge Weldon had disappeared. But Files suddenly took renewed concern.

"Now what?" he demanded. "The Counselor is heading this way — and he must be coming here! And with no less a man than our esteemed Balbriggan with him, who, if you don't know it, Tom, happens to own the Big C Mine."

They entered the room a minute later, then stopped at sight of Shannon. Plainly, they had not expected Files to have any clients. Balbriggan was a nervous-appearing man, quick and bird-like in his movements, while Desseltyne, the Counselor at law, as

his shingle proclaimed, was almost pontifi-
cal in manner. Shannon reached for his hat.

"I'll see you later, Ned," he said, and
turned toward the door, but Balbriggan
stopped him.

"Don't rush off on our account," he
protested. He held out a hand. "Aren't you
the controversial Mr. Shannon?"

Shannon shook hands nodding.

"I guess that describes me," he agreed.

"You and I seem to be in the same boat,"
Balbriggan said, and grinned. "In addition
to others, we have judge trouble. What I
mean is, the judge seems prejudiced against
both of us. That seems to give us something
in common. So it was my idea that perhaps
you, Mr. Files, and Mr. Desseltyne might
work together. On the theory that two heads
are better than one."

The Counselor nodded gravely.

"That is sometimes helpful," he conceded.

"The trouble in my case is that Judge Weldon thinks I'm an imposter," Shannon said.
"I can hardly blame him for that."

"He can hardly think that of the Big C
Mine," Balbriggan said dryly. "Since it was
the original in this part of the country. But
the Dusky Lady steals our ore, ties us up
with injunctions and all sorts of legal red
tape, and there isn't, apparently, a thing that

118

we can do about it. Every decision favors our rival. We can do nothing right, just as they can do nothing wrong."

"In other words, you feel that the judge is prejudiced in their favor?" Shannon asked.

Balbriggan arched his eyebrows humorously.

" 'Prejudiced,' is certainly a mild word for it," he agreed. "I've felt like using stronger."

"But how can he steal your ore?" Shannon asked, perplexed. "I don't know anything about mining laws, but that sounds as though it would be hard to do."

"I'm supposed to know something about mining laws — with the assistance of able attorneys," Balbriggan sighed, sitting down and crossing his legs. "And I agree with you that to steal ore from under our noses sounds as though it should be hard to do. In fact, I would have said it was impossible. But the Dusky Lady is mining, and shipping, a lot of rich ore. Which doesn't come from the Dusky Lady properties. They steal it from us. But how they do it — that's what I'd give a lot to know."

Shannon's interest sharpened. Reading it, Balbriggan went on.

"Mining laws are queer things. For instance, if you own a claim here and I own a claim adjoining it, that doesn't necessarily

119

mean that either of us owns all the ore under our claim, straight down. That would seem to be the logical way, but suppose I find a rich vein of ore on my property, and the vein runs off on to yours somewhere deep underground. According to the law in this state, I, as the original discoverer, have the right to follow that vein through your holdings, and on beyond them, if necessary."

"And is that what the Dusky Lady is doing to you?"

Balbriggan smiled wryly.

"That's what they *claim* they're doing," he agreed. "Since that is the law, I would have no quarrel with it if it was so. But it happens that we are the original discoverer of the vein, not them. And there's a lot of other dark doings far below the surface. I'm convinced that there's not a trace of ore on the Dusky Lady properties, and never was. They simply steal from us. If it could be aired impartially — say a neutral commission go and have a look at all operations, to find out the truth — we'd gladly abide by whatever they found."

"But you can't get such a ruling?"

"Far from it. We're even barred from some of our own property by injunctions. I still can't see how they can steal from us, knowing where their mine is, however. They simply couldn't get in to our vein from there. It's impossible. Yet they are taking ore out every day — and we haven't been able to find out how, or to stop them, legally or otherwise. It's the devil of a situation."

"The wagons do come from the Dusky Lady, though?"

"Oh yes. Loaded with ore which matches ours exactly. And their crew goes into the Dusky Lady to work. They put on a good show — up to the point of allowing any unbiased inspection. Meanwhile they're gutting our properties, somehow, robbing us of a fortune. And we're so tied up that we can't even get out our own ore! They have us on the verge of bankruptcy."

Here was a situation which in some respects paralleled his own. Shannon's interest was mounting. But it might be better to say nothing of his own suspicions until he was able to verify them. He stood up again.

"Maybe we'll be able to work together in some way," he said. "If we can, I'll be glad to."

He descended to the street, more troubled than before by the implication in regard to Judge Weldon. Those were nasty insinuations against a man in his position, and the worst of it was that they seemed justified.

And yet, despite Weldon's animosity toward himself, Shannon found himself pitying, almost liking the man. There was something badly wrong here.

He had done nothing toward solving the problem of Arrow. Unless that fifty thousand dollars was paid when due, he could foresee the pattern which would be followed. It would be revealed that this bogus Shannon was the real mortgage-holder, and the crew from Thunder River would attempt to move in and take over. That would furnish a legal pretext for what he intended to do in any case.

Rejoining Nancy, they went to a restaurant, and there, as the rules required all customers to do, Shannon unbuckled his gun-belt and left it at the door. He noticed that a couple of the crew from Thunder River Ranch were eating there as well, but since they had followed the same rule, their presence did not worry him.

The food was of no such quality as George had dished up, out on the trail. But Shannon was not thinking about what he ate. Nancy, despite their worries, was most agreeable company, and she seemed entirely confident.

"I don't know what they'll be trying, next," she said. "But of course there'll be something. He's that sort — like a rat, always nibbling around the edges. But Dad always enjoyed a good fight, and I guess I'm something like him. We aren't licked yet."

They finished a leisurely meal, the talk drifting far afield from Arrow and its problems. Shannon retrieved his gun-belt, buckled it on again, and they went outside. The air seemed warmer, with a new softness to it, since they had reached town. Nancy nodded wisely.

"We're in for a thaw," she said. "And it's not far off."

That was scarcely encouraging news. Once the snow grew soft, it would be impossible to continue the hunt for the stolen herd, deep in the hills. Even if found, moving them out of that back country would be much more difficult.

As though conjured up by his thoughts, he saw the other man who had called himself Shannon step out of a saloon, then turn toward them, flanked by a couple of his men. Something stirred in Shannon's mind. Where had he seen the fellow before? On Thunder River Ranch and here in town, of course — but before that? He knew, suddenly and quite definitely, that there was something familiar about him, if only he could remember.

Plainly his rival was in a truculent mood, with the triumph of recent victories in his blood. He stopped in front of them, planting himself to block their progress.

"How are you, Miss Nancy?" he asked, pointedly ignoring Shannon. "What's this I hear about you losin' a herd of cattle?"

"I'm sure I wouldn't know what you're hearing," Nancy retorted. "Though I wouldn't doubt that your crew have made a full report to you."

The other man colored as the meaning of this came to him, but he chose to ignore that part of it.

"Any time things don't go right, I can fix them up for you," he said. "All you've got to do is just say the word. You know that, don't you, Nancy?"

"There are cheaper ways of throwing Arrow away than by marrying you," Nancy snapped. "That's something that I'll never do."

Rage was in the man. Shannon could see it getting the better of him, but he swung now to turn it on Shannon, eyeing him with an open contempt in his eyes.

"I suppose you mean by that that you like the looks of this feller better'n me," he sneered. "A man who ain't even got a name of his own, but has to try and steal a better man's."

"You speak as an expert on the subject, I suppose?" Shannon asked.

"Yeah. I've helped lynch more'n one thief — and I aim to pull on the rope of some others, 'fore I'm through with it!"

The animosity and challenge were unmistakable. Shannon cursed the man, under his breath. He'd known another man once, of the same ilk — a man who would try to pick a fight, with two gunmen to back him, and at a time when Shannon was with Nancy. It was a cowardly trick, but he was saved the need for action by the calm voice of Sheriff Pesky.

"Reckon there's a lot o' fellers must feel the same as you do — about wantin' to pull on some ropes," he observed, strolling up, looking more than ever like a mild little fat man who would have no acquaintance with violence. "The things that have been happenin' in this country, kind of riles some of us, that I'll admit. But I won't have no lynchin' — nothin' like that."

"That was just a way of speakin'," the other man said quickly — almost too quickly. "But I'm glad you're here, Mr. Pesky. I been wantin' to see you — and you wait," he growled at Shannon, as he started to brush past. "You're in on this."

Pesky looked mildly interested.

"What's on yore mind?" he demanded.

"One of my crew's been missin', the last couple of days," the bogus Shannon explained. "You know him, I guess. Fred Vit."

"I've seen him," the sheriff admitted shortly.

"Well, I don't like his not showin' up. Vit, he told me that he'd known this hombre here, who claims to be me, back a few years, down Abilene way. Vit says he saw him run out of town there by the law. And that he was going under the name of Prouty at the time."

Shannon did not bother to reply. The sheriff seemed unimpressed.

"Yeah?" he asked.

" 'Course, that ain't neither here nor there," the other Shannon went on. "What I'm interested in is, what's happened to Vit? He was tellin' me that if he ever tangled with this Prouty, there'd sure be trouble, since Prouty would likely remember him. Vit was deppity marshal there at the time."

"I don't believe a word of it!" Nancy flashed.

"Neither do I — about yore Fred Vit bein' a deppity marshal," the sheriff said calmly. "Only contact with the law he ever had, I reckon, would be on the other side of the fence."

The man from Thunder River colored angrily.

"That's as may be," he growled. "But I say it again, I'm wonderin' *why* he's disappeared? I'm just tellin' you the background. And it seems to me that it's yore job, as sheriff, to take some int'rest in such things."

Bill Pesky shrugged.

"I ain't a nursemaid for growed men," he said flatly. "You give me some real thing to go on, and that's different. But it's got to amount to something."

"Yeah? All right. I've been tellin' you what I suspicion. And here's something to mebby even make you set up an' take notice. Looks to me like that gun this Prouty's packin', right now, is the one that Fred Vit had when I saw him last. There's a V, filed on the shank of the butt — and it sure looks like that same V to me!"

Contemptuous, then half-startled, Shannon glanced down at the holstered gun, and unease grew in him. He had buckled on his gun-belt when it was handed back to him, there in the restaurant, with scarcely a glance at it. But this gun, he saw now, was not his own, though very much like it. And that V of which his enemy spoke was plain to see.

ELEVEN

Sheriff Pesky was craning his neck, much like a curious magpie. Shannon, after a moment, pulled the gun from its holster and extended it to him.

"Looks like he's right about the V, Sheriff," he admitted. "But I never saw the gun before. I took off my holster and belt in the restaurant there, as they require, and I didn't take any special look when they handed it back. Seems now as though I was careless."

That, he knew, must be the explanation. One of the Thunder River riders had made the substitution while he ate, doing it either by stealth or with the connivance of the clerk in charge. But while that must be the truth, he knew that it had a weak sound to it. His enemy sneered openly.

"Are you going to be bamboozled by a yarn like that, Sheriff?" he demanded. "Here my man Fred Vit disappears, and like I say, they was old-time enemies. Then *he* turns up, packin' the gun that Fred had the last time anybody saw him. Sounds mighty funny to me."

The sheriff examined the gun with the look of a bird which has discovered an unwanted kind of worm. Then he shrugged.

"That's right interestin'," he observed. "Just like the way the sun, comin' up behind ye, 'll cast a long shadder before." With which rather ambiguous remark, he handed back the gun, turned and sauntered off.

Shannon hid a grin. Plainly, the sheriff had no intention of pulling any chestnuts out of the fire. But this was not the end. It was merely one more seed in the crop which his rival was sowing.

"Looks like we need us a new sheriff in this county!" he now proclaimed loudly. "Though there ought to be law enough to handle things. If there ain't, we'll see that there is!" With that half voiced threat, he too moved in the opposite direction.

Watching him, Shannon was again conscious of the feeling that he had known this man before, that he had seen that peculiar swaggering walk. He was moody as they rode toward the Arrow. And then, like the shell swinging into place for the firing pin as the cocking hammer moves the cylinder, it clicked in his mind. Waldron Cowles!

He sucked in his breath, not believing. Cowles! It was a fanciful, impossible notion. For Cowles was dead — dead and buried at least two years, back in Abilene!

But then he knew that, despite all the evidence to the contrary, he was not mistaken. Cowles had unwittingly given him the clue he needed in that talk about Abilene.

Cowles had been killed resisting arrest, and he, Shannon, had been one of the posse. He hadn't killed Waldron Cowles himself, but he had had a lot to do with running him down after he had robbed a bank and terrorized the town. Shannon had seen the outlaw sprawling in a pool of blood, had known of his being buried the next day. All of that had seemed complete and final.

But strange things happened in such a wild cowtown as Abilene. It was possible that Cowles had been badly wounded, but not dead. Certainly the lawless element there was a large one, and they often worked together. Some other dead man might have been substituted at the burial — bodies were plentiful enough! — or perhaps the box had held no body at all. Given a chance to recover and get out of town, to start life anew under a fresh identity, with the law no longer on his trail — it would be a good trick.

And the evidence that such a thing had

been worked in some way was the fact that this man who now masqueraded under his own name, was that same Waldron Cowles! Shannon was sure of it. He hadn't recognized him at first for several obvious reasons, the chief one being his belief that Cowles was long dead. The second reason had been almost as good, the radical change in the outlaw's appearance.

Back in Abilene he had worn a heavy beard. Now he was smooth-shaven. Yet, visualized without that hair, he was the same. The walk, the way of talking, an arrogance of gesture — they all fitted. And here was an added motive, beyond greed, for a man who sought his full and complete ruin. Cowles had hated him long before the day he had supposedly died. He had blamed Shannon above all others for trailing him and running him down after the bank robbery. Vengeance would have been a driving factor with him.

Shannon had left Abilene soon after the shooting, drifting on. Probably it had taken a long time for Cowles to recover, and then to pick up his trail. But finally he had caught up — in time to trace him to Poncas and to learn of his inheritance of Thunder River Ranch. Always a smooth schemer, Cowles had seen the inherent possibilities in the situation and had acted accordingly.

His one miscalculation had been in supposing Shannon as dead as Shannon had thought him, some years before. As he had turned up from the dead to plague Shannon, so had Shannon come back to claim the ranch. Now, becoming apprehensive, Cowles was resorting to every trick in the book in his effort to get rid of him.

Shannon smiled to himself. Doubt had given way to certainty. The only trouble was, that he saw no way to prove it to the law. Waldron Cowles was officially dead and buried. Shannon's word against his own, under the present circumstances, would carry little weight.

The wind was rising, blowing out of the southwest. It held a chill in its teeth like that of a lady who frowns before she smiles. Shannon did not need Nancy's word for it to know what was coming. He had seen chinook winds work their miracle before. They blew with a breath seemingly cold, but the snow melted under it as they swept across the land.

"It's here!" Nancy said. "Wait until morning!"

The morning brought full confirmation. When going to bed, the wind had seemed almost frigid. But during the night it had carried warmer air from the south, so that Shannon awoke to a summer-like feel and the sound of eaves dripping. Outside, the sun was trying to shine through a broken cloud field, and the snow was mushy underfoot. Little pools were appearing, the beginning of rivulets in spots where the snow was not too deep.

By mid-morning a fresh phenomenon showed, here on Arrow. Though the snow was sinking fast everywhere, it still absorbed most of its own water and held it, not quite able to break loose. But much of the level ground on Arrow, close to the river, was now bare, and the succulent cured grass of the previous season showed plain. It was the first ground that had been visible in many months.

"It's always that way here," Nancy said. "That strip is clear of snow two or three days ahead of anywhere else in the country."

Apparently they were not the only ones to observe it. It had been impossible to do a great deal that day, the snow being too soft for much travel. Shannon had cudgeled his brains in an effort to find some solution to their problem, but without success. Now, just as darkness was settling, he looked out to stare in amazement.

A big herd of cattle was crossing the river.

Thunder River cattle, being driven across the ice by several riders.

As soon as they reached the open grass they fell to grazing hungrily, and the riders turned disdainfully and rode back to the far side of the river. Some among the crew had wondered if this was their missing herd being returned, but Shannon, after the first look, had entertained no doubts on that question. Now he rode to have a look, and the brands confirmed his guess. These were Thunder River stock. Slim, who had thrown a saddle on a horse and followed, swore in exasperation.

"Talk about gall!" he said. "That hombre who goes by your name could give a government mule pointers! It's easy to see what he aims at! He figgers he's got Arrow for sure, and here's some good grass handy. Likewise, he's short of feed. So he just pushes this bunch over here, and is darin' us to do anything about it!"

Nancy had joined them by now. She was almost crying with rage and frustration.

"They're waiting over across the ice, on Thunder River ground, to watch us!" she pointed out. "If we try to drive them off, we'll have a battle on our hands! And by morning the water will be so deep that it can't be crossed — several inches over the ice. Then the ice will go out next. He figures that we'll have to feed his cattle here till he takes the ranch over!"

"If he wants a fight, we can give it to him!" Slim urged. "I'm for pushin' 'em back faster'n they came across!"

Shannon shook his head.

"They'd be hard to move now, anyway," he pointed out. "They're hungry, and that grass tastes like candy to them. Let's get some sleep. Mebby our neighbor has over-reached himself, this time!"

He spoke calmly, but he could not quite keep the excitement out of his voice. He was up at daybreak. The first look out of the window was confusing, for it was a gray world which seemed to swirl and tumble. Fog! But a further look convinced him that it had been right. It was still warm, and the thaw was on in full swing.

The snow had absorbed water like a sponge all the previous day and during the night, holding it back until it could contain no more. Now, under the influence of the continuing thaw, everything was letting loose, all at once. Many more bare spots were appearing. Tiny rivulets were joining forces to make sudden rushing creeks where none had been before. Ponds were spreading to make lakes.

Though he could not see them, Shannon could hear at least two waterfalls leaping from the heights. The streams shoved angrily through a slush no longer able to withstand the pressure. Everywhere these new currents converged on Thunder River. A foot of water flowed above the ice, quickening, deepening by the minute.

A shadowy figure came through the fog to stand beside him. Nancy, with the sparkle of excitement occasioned by this yearly miracle glowing in her eyes.

"The ice will break up before the day's over," she exclaimed. "The river will run free tomorrow, except for ice jams! But we'll have no visits from the other side for a few days now!"

She spoke triumphantly, then her eyes clouded at sight of a few of the invading herd, hungrily grazing.

"But there's no way of getting them back now, either," she sighed.

"That's fine," Shannon nodded. His tentative plan of the evening before was mature now. The fog was an unlooked-for-boon. "Get ready to ride, boys," he instructed. "We're movin' them down-river!"

"And time the fog lifts, we'll have 'em far enough along, and back beyond the timber and hills, to be out of sight," Slim added.

"So *he* can wonder for a spell what we've done with his bunch!"

"That's it," Shannon agreed, but he did not explain that it was only a part of his plan. It worked as Slim had prophesied, however. By the time the fog gave way before the sun, they were far enough along to be hidden from view from the far side of Thunder River. But Shannon kept pushing steadily during the day.

Again the next day they went on, still heading downriver. He was conscious of the curious looks from those of the crew whom he had brought along on this drive, but they no longer asked questions. Late that afternoon they reached Twin Buttes.

As he had counted on, their approach had been observed long before they reached the town, and various men rode out for a look. Among them was Mart McCreedy.

"Hi, Shannon," he greeted. "Nice lookin' bunch you've got here. And Thunder River beef too, I see."

"That's the kind you said you'd prefer to buy," Shannon pointed out.

"Yeah." McCreedy eyed him sharply, as Slim was also doing. "They for sale?"

"If the price is right," Shannon agreed carelessly.

McCreedy grinned, suddenly.

"There'll be no trouble there," he said. "And like I told you before, Shannon, there's no doubt in my mind that you are the right Shannon. But buyin' cattle is a business, you understand. And I like the looks of a jail better from the outside."

"As Tom Shannon, I'll give you a bill of sale for this herd," Shannon suggested.

"That's fine — as far as it goes. But I'm scared they'd tell me I knew I was buyin' stolen property."

"There are tricks in all trades," Shannon reminded him. "I'll give you the bill of sale, and you will give me a receipt, but the money you will pay to Bill Pesky's deputy who resides in this town. Likewise getting his receipt. He will keep the money until matters are settled one way or the other. But his receipt will show that he has it before the dead-line against Arrow, ready to turn over to the court whensoever they tell him to. So long as he holds it, nothing can be done to take over Arrow."

McCreedy was beginning to smile.

"Go on," he urged.

"We will require that he impound the money in a local bank until full proof of the ownership of this herd is established, before payin' it over to anyone. That protects you, McCreedy, for if the court so orders, it can

138

go to my rival, for the herd. You'll be safe. But if they tie a mine like the Big C up with injunctions, so can this money and the mortgage against Arrow be handled the same. Are you willing to buy now?"

McCreedy exploded in a shout of laughter.

"Come on and we'll fix it up," he agreed. "And if I was as sure of heaven as I am that this ranny who calls himself Shannon will never have the spendin' of a cent of that money, sure and I'd be a happy man!"

■ ■ ■ ■

PART III
THE SECRET OF THE
MINE

■ ■ ■ ■

TWELVE

Shannon was elated as he rode northward again with the others of the crew. Cowles had over-reached himself there, and the immediate threat to the Arrow was removed. That helped, for his first duty was to Nancy, who had trusted him, aiding him when he had been up against it. His thoughts dwelt pleasantly on her for a moment. It had been years since he had known a home, but Arrow was like home, and he knew that it was because she waited there. Some day —

But the war went on, even if a battle had been won, And if there was to be a final victory, the fight must be pressed on a larger front, and without delay. He had no illusions as to how crafty or unscrupulous an opponent they faced.

As they neared the vicinity where Thad Gormley lived in seclusion, Shannon sent the others on ahead, then swung off toward the cabin. He was anxious to see his friend again, and he owed it to him in any case.

He was nearing the clearing before he sensed that something was wrong, and spurred suddenly ahead. Then, coming in sight, he pulled up in dismay. Where the cabin and barn had stood were only smoking ruins — and not even much smoke ascended.

Thad Gormley was there, as though he too had just returned from a ride to find this. He stood, a stricken look on his face, the squirrel frisking anxiously about his shoulders as though trying to explain what had happened. The doctor turned at sound of the horse, and stared unseeingly for a moment. His face relaxed as he recognized Shannon.

"Tom!" he said.

Shannon was off his horse now, to put an arm about his friend's shoulders.

"What's happened, Thad?" he asked. "Who's done this?"

Gormley shook his head.

"I don't know," he said, speaking as though dazed. "I was away, since early in the morning, and I — I just got back, a little while ago. It — it couldn't have been an accident. I didn't leave any fire."

"No, it wasn't an accident," Shannon agreed grimly. "I'm afraid maybe it's my fault, Thad. I was talking to Judge Weldon, and he asked who had taken care of me. I didn't know how he felt about you, till after I'd mentioned your name."

A look of pain crossed the doctor's face at Weldon's name, but he shook his head.

"I know he doesn't like me, but he wouldn't do a thing like this," he protested.

"No," Shannon conceded. "I don't think he would. But he's in the power of other men, these days. Unscrupulous men. I'm sure of that. They hate me. And they might have found out from him about you. Maybe they aimed to strike at me, through you."

Absently, playing an old game, Gormley tossed a nut for several feet to the side. The squirrel, which had been waiting expectantly, gave a long jump and grabbed it almost as it landed.

"Strike at you?" Gormley repeated. "But I don't understand. Are you having more trouble, Tom? I thought you'd be settled on your ranch —"

"I was forgetting that you wouldn't have heard any news," Shannon confessed, and gave a brief account of what had happened since the day he had ridden on from here. Gormley listened in amazement.

"That makes several puzzling matters clear," he said. "But I didn't dream that you'd run in to so much trouble. If I had, I'd have gone along with you."

"Then you'd better go along with me, now," Shannon suggested. "I still need your help." Seeing the dismay on the doctor's face, he went on urgently.

"You can't stay here, now. And since they want war, we'll give it to them. This whole situation is a lot bigger proposition than I ever dreamed of, at the start. You, or me, or even Thunder River Ranch, are just a small part of it."

Gormley hesitated, his face flushing painfully.

"Of course I want to help you out, if I can, Tom," he agreed. "And it's kind of you to offer me a place. But I — well, it's just that I'm not used to being with people any more. I've lived alone here so long — with such a feeling about meeting anyone else — What I mean, this is the only sort of place I fit in, any more, or that I'm fit for —"

"Nonsense," Shannon protested. "You'll fit in with people as well as ever. And before we're through with it, the people there in Vermillion are going to find out what fools they've been, and ask you to come back. You'll be welcome on Arrow, Thad. And I do need your help. How about it?"

"When you put it that way, of course I

can't say no," Gormley agreed simply. He looked about regretfully. "Fortunately, I had my pets along with me, and I'll bring them along. Can't leave them to shift for themselves until the weather becomes more settled. So I guess there's nothing to keep me here."

They rode on to the Arrow, and there was a new, fighting jut to Gormley's chin which had not been there before, as he looked back. This was going too far.

One thing puzzled Shannon. How had anyone gotten across the river, still at flood stage, to do this? He had no doubt that the trouble stemmed from Vermillion and had been directed by Cowles, aimed indirectly at himself. The fact that someone had crossed the river made him uneasy.

The doctor was shy when they arrived, but Nancy quickly put him at his ease, along with his pets. The squirrel was a trouper, unafraid of anyone, but the mouse and the lark were slower to gain confidence. Before supper was over they had adjusted to the situation, and Gormley was talking with the rest of them, with almost a pathetic eagerness for the society of his fellowmen again. Nancy was elated at the way Shannon had turned Cowles' trick back on himself, in regard to the herd.

"There's no trace of our herd, yet," she confessed. "But they say that a fair trade is no steal. Except, of course, that this herd really belonged to you in the first place."

"We'll see that he pays the bill, before we get through with him," Shannon promised.

The river was still at flood stage, with considerable driftwood and some ice in its current. The break-up had been spectacular, but now most of the snow was gone from the level country. That in the mountains was beginning to loosen, and with the frost also going out of the ground, there was danger of slides and falling rock.

Shannon had that in mind as he rode among the hills up-river the next day. He was hopeful but not expectant of finding anything new. It was with surprise that he saw his horse raise its head and, looking where it did, observed another horse and rider coming around the shoulder of the hill, not two hundred yards distant. The other man was Sheriff Pesky.

Here was more proof that there were places to get across the river now that the worst of the flood was past. Shannon waved, and waited, expectantly. He had been about to turn back, for, while only a little distance separated them in actual space, there was an almost unbridgeable gap between.

148

The trail which both of them had been following ran along the side of a hill, and its slope was steep. Just above the path, made originally by wild animals and pounded deeper by cattle, rose sharply upthrusting cliff, with a few pine trees and stunted bushes clinging precariously in clefts and cracks. Down below, the hill fell away abruptly for a quarter of a mile, save for a coulee ahead and between them. Flood water of some previous season, tearing down the slope, had gashed here in ragged fashion.

The cattle using the trail had made a path through the coulee, but it was not an inviting one today. A dirty looking snowdrift, up above, melted in the sun, with water dripping down. Small stones rattled away under its influence, and to the experienced eyes of both riders, crossing from one side of the coulee to the other seemed precarious. Not over eighty feet separated them, but any movement across that restricted area might easily loosen a slide which would sweep horse and rider to doom on down below.

Both of them pulled up. Sheriff Pesky studied the situation with a mild interest, stuffing tobacco into the bowl of a stubby pipe. He got this alight and puffed contemplatively.

149

"You comin' acrost?" he queried finally.

Shannon shook his head.

"Guess not. I don't like the looks of it."

"Does look kinda bad, for a fact," Pesky sighed, and added plaintively, "I was hopin' you would. Save me the trouble."

Shannon's interest quickened.

"How so?" he asked.

Smoke wreathed the sheriff's white head to add to his cherubic appearance, an effect somewhat spoiled by his action in removing the pipe and spitting.

"I got a warrant here to serve on you," he explained.

"It's a danged nuisance. Chargin' you with killin' Fred Vit. That's one o' the mean parts o' bein' a law officer. You get all sorts of jobs that you don't like. But a man has to do what he's hired for, like it or not."

This was a gentle warning to him to get away, if he felt so inclined. Shannon understood that, for there had been no need for the sheriff to state his business with that bad spot of trail still between them. He could escape, if he wanted to — for the time being. On the other hand, he knew beyond any doubt that the mild-mannered law man would keep after him until he got him, in such a case. He was playing the game fairly, according to his code.

Fred Vit was the man whom Cowles had claimed was missing, then had charged Shannon with having his gun. The pattern was clear.

"I suppose this other fellow that uses my name, showed you a body?" he asked.

"Yeah," Pesky conceded. "Way back in the hills, with a bullet in his back. Speakin' un-official, it don't make sense to me that anybody'd kill a man and *then* take his gun an' pack it open. I said as much to the judge. But he's sorta prejudiced, and anyway he didn't have no choice but to issue a warrant when this other Shannon swore it out. No more'n I do about servin' it."

"How'd you get across the river?"

The sheriff waved vaguely.

"There's a crossin', up stream a ways," he explained. "Not too bad."

Shannon was thinking hard. If he allowed himself to be arrested and lodged in jail at Vermillion, he would stay behind bars. The judge was sufficiently prejudiced against him that he would not allow bail, since the charge was murder. In any case, it seemed that Weldon obeyed the orders of two men — the boss of Thunder River Ranch and the owner of the Dusky Lady mine. Which made a strange combination.

On the other hand, if he resisted arrest he

would automatically place himself outside the law, which was exactly what Cowles wanted. Either way, his enemy figured to put him in a bad spot.

"You sure you ain't coming over here?" Pesky asked, having allowed a proper time for consideration.

Shannon shook his head again.

"Looks too dangerous to me — even if you weren't over there," he said. "It wouldn't take too much to start a bad slide."

"Might be," the sheriff admitted. But he knew, as did Shannon, that this was the only feasible trail anywhere near. Otherwise it would require a circle of miles, down the river. "Guess I haven't much choice," he concluded, and urged his horse ahead.

The cayuse moved gingerly, tossing its head, stepping lightly, not liking it any better than did its rider. Shannon waited, forced to admire the casual way in which Pesky went ahead with the performance of duty, however disagreeable or risky it might be. He was certain of three things. That Pesky was his friend, that as a law officer he was a square shooter, and that he would do his duty regardless of either danger or personal inclination.

He had covered half the distance when it happened. The action of frost and thawing over a period of days, coupled with the undermining water coming down from the snow-bank above, had poised several tons of earth as on a hair-trigger. The weight of horse and rider now was enough to pull that trigger, and with a startling suddenness a section of earth a score of feet in diameter began to slip. It moved smoothly, not fast at first, but gaining momentum.

There is nothing more terrifying than to feel one's self caught in the grip of a greater and inexorable power which can neither be placated nor controlled. The pony which Sheriff Pesky rode was ordinarily a steady beast and dependable, but it had been skittish of this trail to start with. Now it reacted instinctively, in a quick frantic effort at survival.

Any cow pony, well trained, can follow a madly running steer and make a split-second turn to either side at the very instant that the steer tries to dodge. Seasoned riders are ready for such lightning shifts, else they would not remain in the saddle. This pony was trained in such turns, but now he outdid himself. With one wild plunging spin he came completely around and started back the way he had come.

The only trouble with this maneuver was that the ground beneath his feet was in poor shape for fancy gyrations. It was sliding out from under the hoofs of the cayuse as it made the turn, causing it to slip and slide wildly, and the combination was too much for any rider, however skilled. Bill Pesky was thrown from the saddle.

An instant later, scrambling wildly, hoofs kicking back a shower of mud, his horse regained the firm footing beyond the radius of the slide. But the sheriff was flat on his face, clawing for a hold on greasy ground which was taking him toward a hundred foot drop-off not far below.

It had happened fast, once it started. But Shannon, watching, had seen the first beginnings of the slide. Having been fearful from the beginning that this would happen, he was prepared. His lariat hung coiled and ready, and he had already untied it. Now he jumped out of the saddle, rope in hand, running.

He would much have preferred to remain on his horse, but that was out of the question. He had to get closer to use the rope, and to push his horse ahead would increase the scope of the slide to include them as well. All the ground hereabouts was trembling on the verge of such a take-off.

His loop shot out as he ran, and it fell about the sheriff's shoulders with smooth accuracy. Pesky grabbed it instantly and clung. But, even though Shannon had left his horse behind, his own running weight had been enough to jigger the queasy earth. As the rope tautened, Shannon felt the ground beneath his own feet start to move in unison with the other.

THIRTEEN

It was a calculated risk which Shannon took, just as the sheriff had known the peril of the trail. Now the odds had swung against both of them.

It required no seer to tell that the ground would keep right on sliding, its speed increasing for the next half-hundred feet, until it plunged over the brink of a rocky ledge and piled up somewhere below, with them hopelessly mixed among a few hundred tons of earth and rock. And that, in its way, would solve the problems which plagued both of them. It would also remove all obstacles from the path of Cowles.

There was a possibility, in Shannon's case, that he might be able to run fast enough to reach safety at the far edge of the slide. Only he'd have to drop the rope and forget the sheriff.

There was a second chance, much slighter

155

in prospect. Somewhat below and a bit ahead of him stood a scrubby pine which had grown stubbornly in an unlikely location. If he could reach it and hold fast, he might save both of them. But the big question was whether the tree would also hold fast.

That seemed the most unlikely gamble of all. The very earth in which its roots were embedded was moving. Everything here would hinge on factors so unpredictable that few men would care to gamble on them. How deep was the slide? Was it only a few inches of surface soil out of which the frost had been drawn, slipping along on a solidly frozen layer beneath? If that was so, the roots might descend deeply enough to withstand the strain. But if the moving ground was a mass deep as the roots —

Running, Shannon headed for the tree, and it was tricky traveling. Just as a swimmer in a strong current must start well upstream and aim to come out far down on the other shore, so did he have to move fast to reach the tree before it was above him and out of reach. To keep his feet and go ahead with the slippery earth accelerating at every step was less than easy.

The tree seemed to be running up hill, proof that it was still maintaining its position. He flung out an arm and caught a branch near the tip, though he had aimed for its center. The rope in his other hand jerked taut. Would the tree stand the added strain?

The issue hung in doubt while the slide kept on and the moving ground slid out from under his feet, leaving him suspended, one hand clutching the branch, the other the rope. It was a pull which he could not long sustain. He heard the ominous crack of a root loosened by the pressure, and the tree leaned slightly toward him.

But now the slide was gone. The frozen ground beneath was swept and slick, and a roar came up from below as the earth tumbled and piled. Planting himself as solidly as possibly, Shannon braced.

"Can you follow the rope up?" he asked the sheriff.

"Yeah," Pesky agreed, wasting no breath in surplus words. Mud and debris had plowed around and over him where he had clung, but he got slowly to his feet, then came up the rope, hand over hand. He edged past Shannon to the tree, then gave him a hand.

With the rope free, Shannon looped the stubby branch of another tree that stood just beyond the radius of the slide, and at his insistence, Pesky worked across to solid ground, and Shannon followed. They were on the side now where Shannon's horse stood, and the break in the trail was more formidable than before.

The sheriff, however, surveyed it cheerfully.

"Have to circle around quite a way to get back," he said. "Leaves me tickled that I can do it."

"Better come along back for some dinner," Shannon suggested.

Regretfully, Pesky shook his head.

"Need to be gettin' back for town," he sighed. "Thanks just the same. And there's usual some sweet mixed with the mud." His face relaxed in a puckish grin for a moment. "I lost that danged warrant somewhere in that slide. Well, I'll be moseyin'. So long."

"So long," Shannon echoed, and watched the sheriff move off down the slope. He had a strong suspicion that the loss of the warrant might have taken some contriving, but he had no quarrel with that.

No one, watching him swing along with the easy stride of a man long accustomed to hills and open space, would have guessed how shaken the sheriff was. Not until he reached his horse again, twisting and climbing for nearly two hours, did he stop. Then, climbing into the saddle, he sighed.

"Guess I ain't as young as I once was," he commented. "You did yore part all right, Socrates — 't wan't your fault I got lost in the shuffle. Still and all, I'll ride back with a more relieved mind than I rode out with."

He returned to the spot where previous experience had taught him that the river could be forded with reasonable safety even at flood-tide, and made his way back to the eastern shore. He was nearing Vermillion when he encountered another rider on the road, and it gave him no lift of the spirit to recognize the bogus Shannon.

As he had feared, this usurper of Thunder River Ranch wanted a word with him. He pulled his horse up, and the sheriff, perforce, had to stop. Cowles' heavy eyebrows lifted.

"I thought you was going out to serve a warrant today," he challenged. "I don't see you bringin' back any prisoner?"

"Nothin' wrong with yore eyesight," Pesky acknowledged. "I ain't."

"Didn't you get across the river?"

"Yeah, I done that, all right. Twice."

"Both ways, eh? But you're comin' back empty-handed."

"Yeah, that's right," Pesky conceded again. "Empty-handed sure describes it. With the

159

frost going out on them hill-trails, I got caught in a slide. Lucky to come out of it alive. Lost the warrant."

Cowles regarded him suspiciously.

"Lost it, eh? Well, you knew he was wanted for murder. Did you have to have a warrant?"

The sheriff's chin jutted stubbornly, for so mild appearing a man.

"Yeah, sure did," he retorted. "When I act as sheriff on my own hook, I go after a man if I want him, and a piece of paper or lack of it don't make a danged bit of diff'rence, mister. On the other hand, when I'm just carryin' out the orders of the court — then I do it accordin' to rooles." His gaze was truculent in turn.

"Meanin' that you didn't want to serve that warrant?" Cowles grunted.

"Meanin' exactly that," Pesky assured him. "I've seen coyotes that suspicioned where a trap was set around a temptin' bait. Smart critter, a coyote — like some folks — and no scruples, like some too. I've watched such a coyote cavort around and do tricks, yappin' like he was a dozen all at once. Keep up an act until he attracted the attention of some fool magpie, that's always on the lookout for an easy livin'. Then the magpie bird'd come and perch on the bait, and peck at it, an' hop around — till pretty soon it landed spang on that hidden trap! After which the coyote, grinnin' from ear to ear, 'd come up and get *his* dinner!"

The sheriff spat.

"I don't go around springin' traps to save coyotes," he added pointedly. "Not on my own."

It might hardly be politic, such an open expression of opinion. Certainly it had not set well, judging by the look on the other man's face. But Pesky hid a grin as he rode on, feeling more at peace with the world than in a long while. After all, he reflected, he wouldn't be here to express such opinions if it weren't for the man against whom that warrant had been directed.

He had gone less than a hundred yards when a pound of hoofs made him look around. Cowles was riding wildly, heading back for town, though he had been going in the opposite direction when they met. He passed Pesky with a black scowl but no word, and thundered ahead. The sheriff sighed.

"Plumb easy to guess where he's going — and why," he informed Socrates. "Well, as they say, you can lead a horse to water, but try an' make a balky mule pull yore hat off your head!"

It was close to sunset. The air was balmy for the time of year, and the wind which had moved in the hills had whispered away to a breeze. A laden ore wagon rumbled down toward the town, and the sheriff watched it with expressionless eyes. The driver was familiar to him, so that he knew the ore to be from the Dusky Lady mine — a very rich load, as were all that were being taken out these days.

And that was a mystery which plagued him, since it was neither reasonable nor easy to explain. True, a big crew of men worked at the Dusky Lady every day, going and coming with blatant ostentation. Yet all the known evidence, added to common sense and a knowledge of the country, made it plain that the ore came from the Big C, not the Dusky Lady. And on the other hand such a thing was manifestly impossible.

For the Dusky Lady was not set close to the Big C on adjoining ground, where it might tunnel off and steal ore. True, there was another mine in that position, which everyone suspected was owned by those who controlled the Dusky Lady. But it was a small outfit and took out little ore. What happened was both unbelievable and impossible, but it continued to work out that way, day after day. Wagon loads of heavy ore were tangible evidence not to be brushed aside.

It was no concern of his, of course. As sheriff, he had been called upon to serve a few injunctions, but that was all. Otherwise the quarrel of the rival mines had not involved him. There had been clashes between the rival crews, he knew. Some had been bloody, but neither side had asked the intervention of the law.

The Dusky Lady was too far distant from the Big C — some two miles — for any shaft to reach Big C properties and steal Big C treasure. If they tried it, the Big C would be ready to fight. It couldn't be done.

That was the logic of it. Yet all the ore matched exactly with the scant amount being mined by Big C, tied up as it now was by injunctions. And there was no such ore — there couldn't be — where the Dusky Lady ostensibly got its loads.

That was the mystery, which plagued others than himself. Aside from the mystery of it, Bill Pesky had never cared. Now he found himself beginning to take sides in his mind. Big C had been called a rich and soulless corporation, and sympathy generally had been with the Dusky Lady. But it appeared to the sheriff that somewhere in this maze the Dusky Lady and this bogus Shannon of Thunder River Ranch were tied up together.

That was enough to cause his sympathies to veer sharply.

Leaving Socrates at the stable, he went home and cleaned up, stopping for a leisurely supper. Then, though it was past regular hours, he went to the court house and climbed wearily to his office. He was not surprised to see that a light still burned in the chambers of Bill Weldon. The judge spent increasingly long hours at his office these days.

Pesky hesitated, then went on toward his own office. He did not feel quite up to meeting his old friend tonight, knowing about how the talk must run. He lit a lamp and replaced the chimney, and was just setting it on a corner of his desk when he heard the shuffling footsteps of the other Bill outside in the corridor. Bill Pesky still walked with a firm step. Bill Weldon had done so, up to a few weeks ago. Of late he shuffled like an old man.

The door opened and the judge came in. In the yellow glow of the coal-oil lamp his face looked haggard.

"Back, are you?" he asked. And the tone was as ominous as the lack of friendly greeting.

"Yeah, I'm back," Pesky conceded, equally wary.

"Shannon was in to see me a little while ago," Weldon went on, and surly anger rippled through his tones. Bill Pesky had heard that same anger turned increasingly on others of late, but until tonight the judge had never used it against him.

"He says you claim to have lost your warrant for this pretender Shannon, and that you refused to go on and arrest him without one," Weldon rasped. "Are you forgettin' your duty as sheriff of this county?"

A hot retort rose to Pesky's lips, but he choked it down.

"Nope," he denied. "I'm not forgettin'."

"Then why didn't you bring him in?"

"Like I told this *pretender* Shannon, I lost the warrant."

The judge's lips thinned.

"A likely story! Anyway, why didn't you bring him in? You're sheriff!"

"As an officer of the court," Pesky answered carefully, "I serve warrants when issued — whether I like the job or not. But aside from that, I'm a duly elected officer and free to use my own judgment as to how to enforce the law. Which I do!"

The judge snorted.

"Oh, I know that you've got a crazy notion that this pretender is the real thing," he growled. "That's poppycock, of course.

165

Anyway, here's a fresh warrant, sworn to by Shannon and issued by me. I expect you to serve it — and to bring him in without delay!"

He extended the paper peremptorily. Pesky eyed it, but he backed away, hands behind his back.

"You can keep it," he said. "I don't want it."

"What?" Weldon choked. "Are you trying to tell me, Bill Pesky, that you won't obey the orders of this court? Do you realize who you're talkin' to?"

Ire had been building up in Pesky over long months. Always he had carefully restrained it, partly for old friendship's sake, and partly because he realized the strain under which the judge labored. But now he boiled over. Reaching out, he snatched the warrant and tore it across and across.

"That for your dummed warrant, Bill Weldon!" he snorted. "I wouldn't be alive to think of servin' it if Tom Shannon hadn't risked his neck — and come dummed near losin' it — to save mine today! He's a man. This other is a trumped-up charge, and you know it as well as I do. As to duty, I'm elected sheriff of this county, elected by the same people who elected you — and responsible to them, not to you! If you want to do your job one way, that's your business. But I do my work as I see fit, and don't go tellin' me how to run my office!"

Weldon glared.

"I could have you locked up for contempt of court —"

"Gum drops an' molasses! Who's to do it? *I'm* the sheriff, that does the lockin' up around here! And let me tell you, Bill Weldon, I got plenty contempt for you as a judge, the way you been actin' lately! We been friends a good many years, Bill, and I used to be proud of it. I don't give my friendship easy, and when I do, it counts for something. But here lately I been plumb ashamed of you. Sure your daughter died — and that was hard on you. Hard on me, too. Didn't she call me Uncle Bill? Wasn't she all I had, same as she was all you ever had? But there's a limit. You accused Thad Gormley of killin' her, and you know he loved her as much as ever you did!

"But that wan't the worst, makin' a fool of yourself that way. You always was an honest man and an upright judge! I aim to be a square sheriff, and no cat's paw for crooks! But it looks to me like that's what you've come to lately. Why you'd be such a fool as to sell out — why you'd do it in any case, I don't know. But I do feel that mebby it's a good thing Louise is dead! It's better so, with her father a crook! She'd turn over in her grave if she knew how you'd slid —"

Bill Pesky stopped, suddenly conscience-stricken. A strange look had overspread the judge's face while he talked. Now, with a strangling sound, Bill Weldon slumped. Pesky sprang to try and catch him, but he was too late as the judge thudded, senseless on the floor.

Fourteen

Cowles' mood, by the following morning, was verging on savagery. He had come to the Thunder River country with two things in mind. The first was to acquire wealth and power, and the means had providentially come to hand for doing this with comparatively little effort on his part. That part of the plan had worked out well.

But he had also had the somewhat vague notion that, once established here, he would play the part of a squire or country gentleman, an urbane sort of individual to whom all others in the community would look up. Just where the idea had first come to him, he had no way of telling. It had seemed a pleasant sort of position, akin to kingship.

But there were pitfalls in the way, disadvantages which he had never dreamed of. It appeared that being urbane and serene were different from lordly and condescending. Maybe his confusion on that point had been the beginning of the trouble. Certainly the others in the valley refused to play their part as he had expected. They seemed to regard him in a light directly opposite to that which he had hoped for.

Even before the arrival of Shannon, he had teetered insecurely on the pedestal he had set up for himself. Since then, matters had gone from bad to worse. The sudden appearance of his old enemy on the ranch, after he had believed him safely dead these many weeks had shaken Cowles more than he liked to admit. The one redeeming point had been his certainty that Shannon had not known him.

But of late he was not even sure of that. He had taken steps to rectify the earlier error in regard to this man whom he feared and hated above all others, but the fellow seemed to bear a charmed life. Nothing worked as it was supposed to.

Word had reached him, early this morning, of the condition of Judge Weldon. Apparently he had suffered a stroke, and it was a moot question as to whether or not he would recover. The medico had said cau-

tiously that it was an unusual case. Once
Weldon recovered consciousness, he might
be nearly normal, or quite the contrary. *A
fool of a doctor,* Cowles thought savagely.
Report had it that this fellow's predecessor,
who had been chased out of town, had
known his business. Certainly this pill-
pusher did not.

The news had filled Cowles with near-
panic. His own continuing position depended to a large extent upon the jurist.

Sight of the sheriff had not been re-
assuring. Bill Pesky had a strained look on
his face today, but it was only too apparent
that he was going to disregard the second
warrant as he had done with the first.
Considering this, Cowles came to a conclusion. What was to be done he must do
himself. There had been a dim yearning in
him to go straight, but each step along a
crooked trail led you deeper into trouble.
This, he saw now, was a trail of no retreat.

The knowledge was rawly oppressive, but
it steadied him. There were new and greater
possibilities for a man who knew how to
grasp them, and do it ruthlessly, as you
must with a nettle. On second thought, the
incapacity of the judge might offer a wider
scope for his operations than before.

He rode out of town, heading north, but

today he did not take the west road leading to Thunder River Ranch. Instead, he followed the road east of the sky-slicing range of hills, toward the mining country. On the way, he passed two heavily laden ore wagons, trundling toward Vermillion. Knowing the drivers, he knew that these belonged to the Dusky Lady, and his mouth watered at sight of the potential wealth rolling past him. His scowl deepened thoughtfully.

The Dusky Lady was, outwardly, much like any similar mine. A large, long warehouse sprawled, crowded close up against the sheerly rising hills. Other and smaller buildings clustered around, like young and forlorn chicks beside an indifferent hen. A shaft dropped away into the depths of the earth, and about it was maintained a spurious scene of activity. On special occasions and for selected audiences, ore was even hoisted out of it. Cowles paid little attention to any of it, for he knew how the trick worked, and this was an old story to him.

Instead he went directly to the mine office, and was presently alone with the superintendent, Jan Lansing. Lansing, as Cowles happened to know, was no more his name that Shannon was his, nor was superintendent an accurate description of his position. But these things had their uses, as no man knew better than Cowles.

Lansing looked up to nod, not too graciously. He was a heavy-built man, with gnarled hands and a perpetual stoop, and he was the owner, possessing in himself the non-existent Company which, being vaguely distant, lent an air of distinction to an enterprise otherwise sadly lacking in glamor. It served as well to postpone occasional embarrassing questions for an indefinite period, on the pretence that they were being referred to a mythical board for action.

"Well?" he asked.

Cowles helped himself, without invitation, to a chair. He elevated his big boots to a position on the desk close beside Lansing's nose, with the spurs just over the edge. He paid no attention to Lansing's look of distaste.

"Heard the news?" he asked.

"What about?"

"Weldon."

"I've heard it."

"Makes a diff'rence — mebby."

"I don't see how," Lansing denied. "Not for the present, anyway."

"Shannon's doing a devil of a lot of snooping."

Lansing shrugged, looking remarkably like a grizzly bear in the process.

172

"That's your lookout," he retorted.

"We're in this together," Cowles reminded him. A gleam of avarice crept back into his eyes. "You're gettin' a hell of a lot of mighty rich ore, these days."

"That's my business."

"It's mine, too," Cowles snarled. "Looks to me like I'm gettin' the little end of the horn."

Animosity had been building up in Lansing as well. Now it burst out of him.

"What you kickin' about?" he demanded. "Your pay was to be the ranch — and you got it. That's damn good money for what you're doing — and you jumped at the chance at the time. If you can get Arrow along with it, that's up to you. You've been throwin' your weight around plenty, lately. But don't try crowdin' me."

Cowles glowered. Only one thing restrained him, and that was a sense of caution. Until Shannon was definitely disposed of and he was sure how things would go, he could not afford a quarrel. If it came to a showdown, they'd need their united strength to survive. Afterward — well, that would be something else again. Cowles lowered his feet and stood up.

"Mebby I was talkin' too much," he conceded. "Things ain't been going good.

173

I'm kinda upset."

"You needn't be," Lansing assured him. "We got the world by the seat of its britches on a down-hill pull. That vein's gettin' richer all the time. And money talks!"

"Yeah," Cowles agreed. "I guess that's right. Well, I'll be moseyin'. Just wanted to make sure you knew about things."

He went outside again, got his horse, and swung into the saddle. But he did not ride back the way he had come. He had other things on his mind, not the least of them being that last remark of Lansing's concerning the richness of the ore. That was exactly what he had suspected, and now greed was uppermost in his mind.

Maybe he didn't need to work this along with Lansing. After all, the vital part of the set-up was in his hands. There would have to come a break, sooner of later. So the sooner it came the more money there would be for his own pockets. He'd take a look around, to study all the angles. And then. . . .

Andy Devine was in a sullen mood also. It had persisted for days now, a gloom which enveloped him like a fog. He was a tall, gawky kid, awkward and given to daydreaming, prone to imagine tense situations with himself as the all-conquering hero who solved them. Prior to the coming of Shannon, it had been easy to dream.

There had been regret in him when the others of the Arrow crew had quit and left the outfit badly in the lurch. Regret for a tough situation. But that feeling had been tempered with pleasure at the result. For the first time it had left him as the only youthful man on the ranch, just as Nancy was young. He had pictured how he would solve all difficulties and earn her warm regard.

There had been one hindrance. Solving the troubles of Arrow was not so simple in reality as in a day-dream. But he had had little chance to show what he could do, he consoled himself now. Shannon had come to spoil his Eden all too soon, then the added crew. He was no longer a person of some importance, the one to whom Nancy would turn naturally for advice and help. He was again just the Kid.

Jealousy was a searing flame in him. The manner in which Shannon had sold that herd of Thunder River cattle and applied the money to the Arrow mortgage made it all the worse. But Shannon had not recovered the Arrow herd!

And there, the Kid decided, lay his great

oportunity to show what he could do! Since they had searched north, south and west, with equally unavailing results, it followed that the herd must be across the river, on Thunder River Ranch itself. And where could a better hiding place be found than that blind canyon back in the hills?

Once Andy had been tempted to speak of the likelihood of the place. Now he was glad that he had not. He'd do this on his own, and share no glory with anyone, least of all with Shannon.

Riding out by himself, Andy had observed the sheriff, at a considerable distance. He had seen where he went to cross the flooded river, and elation had grown in him. If an old has-been like Pesky could cross at flood-stage, he would have no trouble in doing so.

It had been too late for a foray that afternoon. But the next morning, early, the kid set out. Since this was a slack season at the ranch, with not much work that could be done, there had been no trouble in getting permission to go and look for sign of the missing herd. He had not bothered to suggest that he intended to look for sign across the river. They could find that out when he told them where the herd was.

He crossed without difficulty, and headed straight east to the hills before turning south. Up close to the mountains, there would be less likelihood of anyone seeing him.

The kid possessed a certain ability when he was alone. Much of his awkwardness was due to self-consciousness, and that vanished when there was no one around. If the stolen herd was back in here, as he was now certain must be the case, they would probably be guarded. Only one or two men would be necessary for that job, but it would pay to go warily so as not to be discovered. Guards would not look with favor on a rider from Arrow.

Choosing a way which followed coulees, the lower slope of ridges and made use of every covering bit of brush or rock, Andy rode. Finally he reached a chosen point and left his cayuse, deep in a coulee. Then he started the laborious task of climbing, to where, somewhere up the mountain, he could look down into the canyon's depths. And from where, if necessary, he could descend for a more careful exploration.

The sun shone brightly, warm with the promise of spring. In sheltered spots a few shoots of grass shone green, and once he found crocus and adder-tongue in blossom. His impulse was to pick them, to give to Nancy on his return. But he put the notion aside, knowing that they would be wilted long before he could get back.

It was already close to noon, and he stopped to eat the lunch he had gotten from Pansy. Presently he reached the selected point and could see down into the canyon, its depths a considerable distance below.

Down there the sun seldom reached, and they were shadowy now. As his eyes grew accustomed to the gloom, Andy's breath quickened with excitement. He was right! He must be, for the snow down in the bottom was trampled, hard-packed. What else than the herd could cause that?

But there was no sign of any of the cattle, and he wanted to be sure. Laboriously he descended, sometimes at the risk of a broken limb. There was snow here, brittle and cold where the sun had not touched, and the slope was steep. He slipped and slid, then stopped, heart thudding, to look and listen, but no sound broke the almost eerie stillness of the place. He slid again, and was on the canyon floor.

Eagerly he scrutinized it, his sureness turning to incredulity. There were hoof-marks here, it was true, but they were not those of cattle. They were bigger — the shod hoofs of horses. And there were wagon tracks as well. This canyon bottom was like a well-used road.

Completely puzzled, the boy started to turn. He was passing a clump of brush when something jabbed painfully into his back, and a harsh voice shattered the last of his dream.

"What do you think you're spyin' about, Kid? Lookin' for somethin' — like a bullet, eh?"

Gasping with the pain of the gun-barrel which seemed almost to drive between his ribs, Andy turned, to stare into the grim-smiling face of the man whom he least desired to see. Shannon, as he called himself — the Shannon who was boss here on Thunder River Ranch.

Already, Cowles was reaching to help himself to the holstered gun which the kid wore, and which he had had no chance of using. As he pocketed it, his smile changed to a scowl.

"Speak up, Kid!" he hissed. "What you lookin' for? Not that I don't know, you sneakin' pup!"

Deliberately, Cowles hit him — a flat-handed blow alongside the head which seemed to have the drive of a bear's paw. Andy's head snapped to the side, so that for a moment he thought his neck was broken. He staggered, tripped on the slippery ice surface, and sprawled full length. A boot drove with renewed viciousness into his stomach, doubling him up in retching pain, the wind all gone out of him.

Terror gripped the Kid. He tried to scream, and could not find the wind. He had an agonized glimpse of the face above him, and felt that he was looking at his doom. But now something caused Cowles to pause in his sadistic punishment, to stand for a moment suddenly alert, listening. It seemed to Andy, watching him, terrified but fascinated, to be the same look as on a coyote's face under similar conditions — crafty, cunning.

All at once Cowles stooped, seizing him by the collar. Then he dragged him back, inside the shelter of the clump of brush. The long barrel of Cowles' revolver was jamming painfully into his still quaking stomach.

"Say what I tell you to, Kid!" he grated, almost whispering. "Yell it out. Now get it! *Help, Shannon! Tom Shannon! He's killin' me!*"

"Yell it," Cowles hissed, and the gun barrel prodded viciously. "Make it good, or it'll be the truth."

Painfully, almost blubbering, the Kid obeyed.

FIFTEEN

Had Shannon been half an hour earlier he would have seen the Kid crossing the river. His destination was the same. As it was, his horse entered the water a short distance lower down than the spot chosen by Andy, and came out farther down on the other side, so that he missed the tracks in the mud.

He chose a somewhat different route to reach the canyon, knowing what his objective was. This was a risky job, but there was vital information which he had to get, and it would be easier and safer working alone.

His plans worked as scheduled until he stood on the bottom of the canyon. Only then did he hear sounds like a struggle from just around a bend. While he hesitated, puzzled, a shout went up — full of agony and terror. The voice of Andy Devine, calling to him for help.

Amazement held Shannon rooted for a moment. He had not guessed that the kid would be on this side of the river, much less here. And how had he known that he was here too, to call for help?

Just as swiftly the obvious answer seemed clear. The Kid had ridden up-river to look for the missing cattle. He must have seen

Shannon cross the stream, and, figuring that the boss would be prowling unfriendly territory and might need help, had followed. Not stopping to think how he might hinder rather than help, Andy had blundered into trouble.

Shannon was annoyed. But all chance of secrecy had already been spoiled. Shannon swung around the bend of the canyon, gun in hand, and stopped, for the road was empty.

Humiliation washed like a wave across the Kid, followed by rage. He had been tricked like the veriest blundering tenderfoot, captured without a fight. Now it came to him what Cowles had been listening for. Strange as it seemed, Shannon must be somewhere close at hand — at least this man believed so. This was a trick to lure the boss into trouble.

There was good stuff in Andy. Jealousy and hatred had rankled in him, but now that peril was imminent he remembered that he and Shannon were members of the crew of Arrow, that this other man was their common enemy. He had done an unforgivable thing, but he would rectify his error even if it killed him. Suddenly he shouted again.

"Look out, Tom! It's a trick!"

He had time for no more, but that was all

that he had hoped for. Cowles kicked savagely, and again his boot drove into the Kid's stomach, doubling him up with agony, so that a moan was torn from his lips. Cowles' voice was ugly.

"Drop that gun, Shannon, or I'll blow his brains out! And do it pronto! I'll count to three!"

Instantly he began to count, with cold precision. Shannon hesitated. He knew now where his enemy was, hidden in that clump of brush. In a shoot-out the odds would be with Cowles, but he would have risked it without hesitation save for the threat. He had no doubt that Cowles would put a bullet through the Kid's head, unless he obeyed.

And no matter how fast he might be with his gun, he'd be too slow to prevent that. He had no sure target at which to aim, while Cowles had only to squeeze the trigger.

One alternative was almost as bad as the other. But it seemed to Shannon that the Kid trailed him here with the intention of siding him if he got into trouble, or helping if he could. It hadn't worked that way, but that did not alter the spirit. Under such circumstances there was only one thing to do. Shannon allowed his revolver to drop, and raised his arms.

"That's being sensible," Cowles grunted. He stepped out into the open, ran his hand quickly over Shannon to make sure that he had no other weapon, and pocketed the dropped gun. Gloating triumph was in his face.

"I thought I heard something, and I just had a hunch that *you* might be snoopin' around, too," he explained. "And that one sure paid off. But you showed mighty poor judgment, bringin' a fool kid on a job like this."

Shannon said nothing. There was no point to confessing that the Kid had done all this on his own account. His mind was going ahead, uneasily, to what would follow. None of it would be good. And the chances of getting out of this fix were so slender as to be virtually nonexistent. This man both feared and hated him, and he would ask no better opportunity for settling old scores once and for all. The main question would be as to method.

Cowles was already pondering that. A body, particularly with a bullet-hole in it, could lead to embarrassing questions later. It was much better to dispose of such details neatly and surely. And now an idea was coming into Cowles' mind as a new sound echoed through the canyon. The hollow rumbling of a wagon, lightly laden. It came from below, in the south branch.

"Stand hitched," Cowles warned, and, not taking his eyes off Shannon, he stepped back to the brush and pulled the still inert figure of the Kid out into the open. For a moment, in sudden wariness, he cast a quick suspicious glance about at the heights in both directions. It was just possible that there were more than the two of them from Arrow fooling around here, though that seemed unlikely. But the possibility made Cowles more eager to get things done.

He left the Kid lying on the hard-packed snow. Andy was just beginning to stir, having lost consciousness in a wave of overwhelming pain at that last kick. Now he moaned, opened his eyes, and tried to sit up, then groaned. In addition to the bad bruise he had taken, at least a couple of his ribs were broken.

"Serves you both right!" Cowles growled. "You sellin' my herd down Twin Buttes way! That was damn smart — too smart for yore own good!"

The thing had rankled, particularly as there had been nothing that he could do about it until the law took its unhurried course, and Shannon and his crew could be disposed of. The knowledge that everyone

185

in Vermillion had been laughing at him, however secretly, had done nothing to sweeten Cowles' temper.

The wagon came in sight around the bend, one of the big, multi-tiered box ore wagons, and stopped in amazement as the driver sighted them. Shannon recognized him. He was the same fellow who had been driving that wagon which had tried unsuccessfully to crowd him off the road, down near Vermillion. But this time the wagon was far above the Dusky Lady, and heading in the opposite direction.

The driver stared, his glance flicking from Cowles to Shannon to the Kid and back to Cowles. Then he grinned.

"Looks like you got him, this time!" he said.

"Looked like it was a chore that I'd have to handle myself," Cowles retorted, bringing a flush to the driver's face. "Get down. I want your help."

"Sure, sure." The other man made haste to obey. Here was confirmation of what Shannon had suspected. These men, who ostensibly worked for the Dusky Lady, took Cowles' orders without question — even on matters involving murder.

"Get a piece of rope, or slice off part of a rein," Cowles instructed. "Tie his hands behind his back — and see that you do a good job." He indicated Shannon.

The rope was found, and Shannon had no choice but to submit. Cowles kept watch with a leveled gun.

"Now tie his ankles," he added. "Tight!"

Shannon was seized from behind, dumped unceremoniously on the ground, and his legs trussed. The driver grinned and looked expectantly.

"Load him inside the wagon," Cowles ordered. "I'll drive it myself."

Still there was no disposition to question his orders. But having loaded Shannon inside the empty wagon box, the driver nodded toward where the Kid sat, looking a picture of dejected misery.

"What about him?" he asked.

"You look after him," Cowles instructed. "Take him back down. I reckon he can walk. He's just a harmless fool. He's to be kept locked up a few days, till things are all fixed up. After that it won't matter."

Cowles climbed to the seat of the wagon and gathered up the reins. The driver, not unkindly, helped the groaning Kid to his feet and started him moving.

It seemed to Shannon that he was in a good position to learn the secret of this canyon and of the Dusky Lady, as he had wanted. But the chances of putting that knowledge to good use after he had it were dim.

Cowles did not seem inclined to talk. He drove glumly, presently passing the guard who watched at the point of the V, turning then up the north branch of the canyon, straight back into the heart of these mountains. Lying on the floor of the wagon box, it was impossible for Shannon to see the road itself, but he could tell that it continued to run quite smooth and passable. Whatever obstacles might once have been in the way had been cleaned out.

Back in here the canyon was like a gash in the hills, so deep that it was nearly dark along the bottom, even with the sun rising toward its zenith. Along here no brush or spear of grass ever grew. But as the dusk grew deeper, Cowles suddenly swore under his breath, manifestly displeased. Then he pulled the team to a stop.

Plainly, he had met someone, and the encounter had taken him by surprise. Just as clearly, it was one whom he would have preferred to avoid.

"Why, uh — hello, Jan," he managed. "Didn't expect to run into you up here."

Lansing came closer now, like a shambling bear, his face smooth of expression — too smooth. He stood to look over the side and into the wagon, and still his face expressed no emotion.

"I like to look around and keep an eye on things," he said. "Is this him?"

"Yeah," Cowles conceded. "I caught him snoopin' around back there. Sometimes it does pay to look around. These guards are too damn careless."

"That was good work," Lansing admitted. He reached up, grasped the spring of the seat, and pulled himself to the hub of a front wheel and so on in to a seat beside Cowles. As the latter clucked uncertainly to the team, he asked a question.

"What you got in mind?"

"We got to get rid of him," Cowles explained. "He knows too much."

"Not much doubt of that," Lansing agreed. "And you've got an old grudge against him, I understand?"

"I'll say I have. He come damn near bein' the cause of my stretchin' a rope, a few years back." A crooked grin replaced the scowl on Cowles' face. "But he done me a good turn, kinda — not that he aimed to. It was while I was lookin' for him, aimin' to pay him back, that I met up with you — and found out about his inheritin' this ranch, and saw the chance to grab it."

"That was a lucky break," Lansing conceded. "This canyon is the real key to our whole scheme." The animosity that had been between them earlier in the day seemed forgotten now, or at least put aside for the moment. "But what do you figure to do with him? What's the plan?"

"It's a beaut," Cowles assured his companion, but for the moment he had no opportunity to explain. The nature of the place had changed abruptly. They were still in the midst of the hills. But where the canyon was supposed to come to a dead end, and had apparently done so in the past, there was a change now. One that had been made, Shannon knew, by these men, directing a crew of experienced miners.

Here was a big enough place for the wagons to turn around. Here too was a chute, built of planks, high enough for a wagon to drive beneath. Such a chute as is used at the entrance to small coal mines in mountain country, with a wooden gate which could be raised to allow a box-full of ore to slide down the chute and into the wagon box.

Leading back into the hill from the chute was a black hole, the mouth of a tunnel or mine shaft. It was equipped with a track and ore cars. Shannon was sure of that as a miner appeared at its mouth, the candle on his cap emerging like a dim moth from the gloomy recesses. He was pushing a loaded ore car down the slight decline, to empty it with a roar into the chute.

A lot of things which he had only suspected before were becoming clear to Shannon now. The mystery of the phantom Dusky Lady — and how the ore of the Big C was being stolen, from under the very noses of the owners, and being done in a way which had seemed completely impossible.

But having verified his own hunch, it looked less and less as though the knowledge would do him any good. There was at least a wagonload of ore in the chute now, waiting for them. Enough to fill the box to the top, a load five feet deep. Cowles drove the wagon under the chute and stopped, kicking the brake on and winding the reins about it. Now, grinning wolfishly, he started to climb back to the lever which raised the gate.

"Yeah, it's a beaut!" Cowles went on. "He's bothered me all he's ever going to, and this'll finish him without a trace. What I'm going to do is load the wagon now. By the time this ore smashes down on top of him, he won't do any more meddlin'!"

"But wait, you fool!" Lansing protested. "When it's shipped they'll find the body. At the smelter, if not sooner. That won't do."

"I got that all figured," Cowles assured him. "We'll take this load out, same as any other. I'll tend to that myself. Only it won't get as far as town. I'll get wrecked, tipped over, there along the river, where the drop-off is deep, in among that thick brush. It'll spill, with him on the bottom. And he'll stay there till kingdom come!"

SIXTEEN

He was again reaching for the dump lever, but Lansing stopped him with a sharp exclamation.

"No! Leave that alone! Whose ore do you think this is that you're wastin, anyway?"

Cowles turned with a quick snarl.

"What does a load of it amount to?" he demanded. "Sure, yours — everything's got to be yours! But where'd you be if it wasn't for me and my land here to make this set-up possible? Besides that, he's just as big a threat to you as he is to me, now that he knows about things."

Lansing restrained himself with an effort, keeping his voice even.

"Likely he is," he agreed. "But I'll take

192

care of that part of it. Do you know how much this stuff is worth? Over a hundred dollars a ton, it's runnin', these days! And there's five tons to a load." Cowles drew in his breath sharply at this revelation, for the sum was surprisingly above what he had supposed it to be. Unnoticing, Lansing went on.

"You ain't got anything to kick about. It was my idea in the first place, and you was plumb tickled at the notion of gettin' the ranch for nothing, just to take over. As for him, like I say, I got a lot better way of handlin' him."

"How?" Cowles demanded.

"Untie his feet, so he can walk. We're going back into the mine. No need to pack him. We can watch him all right."

Cowles hesitated, then shrugged and complied. Shannon had listened in silence, hopeful but not very expectant. They discussed the business of disposing of him as callously as the disposition of a stray cow. The one chance that he could see which might work in his favor was a quarrel between these two, but their very greed held them together in the pinches.

It was a relief to be able to use his legs, though his arms were still tied behind his back, so tightly that they were growing half-numb. From a small cubby-hole sort of office building beside the chute, Lansing produced a couple of miner's caps and lit the candles. With these flickering and giving a weird, unsteady light, the three of them turned back into the tunnel through which the ore car had come. Lansing led the way, Cowles behind, Shannon stumbling between them.

The tunnel rose in a slight incline, making it easy for the loaded ore cars to run down, but not so steep but what they could be pushed back empty without much trouble. Much of this tunnel had been dug or blasted through solid rock. A slight draft seemed to go through it, assuring ventilation and good air.

It did not go far, perhaps a couple of hundred yards, then its nature changed. No miner himself, and strange to such mole-like burrows, Shannon could sense the difference. That tunnel had been dug for just one purpose, to get to a destination, to afford an outlet. It was no mine shaft. But here, ahead, were those of a real mine.

At this point a good sized underground room had been hollowed out. Boxes and tools and various other equipment were piled or stacked around at the sides, and several holes or shafts led off at various angles. One of them appeared to be the main one, in regular use, and the line of narrow track led straight back into it and disappeared. Faint sounds echoed ghostily from somewhere along in its recesses.

Here, Shannon realized, was the answer to the mystery of the Dusky Lady. It was evident that Lansing was not only an experienced miner, but a skilled engineer. But, like Cowles, he was a crook by preference, and the richness of the Big C mine had been a temptation.

Stealing the ore of such a going concern, however, was no simple matter. Even with the laws which permitted following a vein of ore already found on your own property, it would have been extremely risky. Particularly since they had been unable to find the vein on any adjoining property.

Any attempt at a crass, outright steal would have been foredoomed to failure. Balbriggan of the Big C and those for whom he ran it would fight back, both in the court and in extra-legal ways, and almost every factor, including money with which to work, would favor them.

But this was a case where two heads had proved better than one. Lansing and Cowles had discovered that possession of Thunder River Ranch would give them the key to unlock this Big C treasure. As a mining man, Lansing had talked with Big C miners and learned approximately how and where the vein of ore ran, until he had been certain that he could bore in from the side and hit it, well ahead of where the Big C men were at work. And the horseshoe canyon here in the hills had given him the chance.

His ability as an engineer had been called into play. A claim had been secured, openly, next to Big C properties, but that was only a blind. Making careful calculations, Lansing had discovered what no one else had ever more than guessed at, that it was not far from the dead end of this upper canyon, on through to the other valley.

In confirmation, Lansing was talking now, with the pride of a man who has made careful calculations and seen them work out as planned.

"Right here is where we struck the old shaft that the Big C had sunk and abandoned," he told Cowles. "They'd been lookin' for the vein when it petered out on them a couple or three years back, and figured it would be around here somewhere. But they didn't find it with that bore, and then the vein got rich again, so they closed off this other and went on. But when I found their old hole, I knew I was hittin' right where I'd aimed for."

"That took some smart figurin', all right," Cowles conceded, almost grudgingly.

"Skill, my boy, skill and know-how. And if I do say it myself, there's no better engineer in the business. After we got in this far, it took only a few bores to find the vein. And Big C is still trying to discover what's happenin' to them. They know well enough, from the looks of the ore that we're shippin', that we're takin' it from their vein. And they know that we're not minin' it from the Dusky Lady, even if it does come out of there. They know we're stealin', but they can't see how. So far, it's never occurred to them that we could hit in from this side, and so far ahead of where they're working."

A few miners worked in the false shaft of the Dusky Lady, purely as a blind. The others, like the ore wagons, passed through a concealed door and followed another tunnel out into the southern branch of the canyon, and so on up here to the actual mine. It had been a daring plan, and it was paying off big.

Cowles was looking around with quickened interest. Apparently he was learning new things which meant a lot to him.

"What's your scheme for getting rid of

him?" he demanded, with a jerk of his thumb.

"A simple one, but effective," Lansing assured him. "There was one serious flaw in your plan, my friend, aside from the waste of good ore. The miners from both outfits know what this ore is worth. Someone would have tried to recover it if we did not, and found what was hidden under it. Nothing like that will ever happen here."

"Mebby you'll get around to tellin' me what it is, when you get through braggin'," Cowles suggested, with heavy sarcasm.

"It's simple. See that old shaft right there at the side? That's one that the Big C dug and abandoned. It goes down, straight, for about a hundred feet, maybe more. I could have told them they wouldn't find the vein that way, but they dug it. It's got some debris in it now that they dumped in, but not much. Ordinarily, we'd have filled it before this, except that we've needed all the waste to fill those holes in the road.

"We'll dump him down it, and start fillin' it up. None of the miners will need know that they're buryin' him when they dump stuff in. We'll get a few loads on top of him yet today. In a little while it'll be filled to the top."

Cowles was silent, considering the plan.

Then he spoke with grudging admiration.

"Sounds good," he agreed.

"It is good," Lansing insisted. "Perfect. And lucky that we're just about ready to fill it in any case."

Shannon listened, grimly silent. In the jouncing wagon he had struggled against his bonds, but the rope had been well-tied. Now, watched by both of them, there was still no chance. Cowles grabbed him by the shoulders and shoved him toward the yawning mouth of the abandoned shaft.

Seen from above, the hole looked as uninviting as the description Lansing had given of it. It was about six feet wide, and seemed to go straight down. With a sudden rush, Cowles sent him stumbling and kicking, headlong and down into engulfing blackness.

Shannon had time for a quick, confused thought of Thad Gormley, of Nancy Adams and Arrow. Particularly of Nancy. If he could get back to them with what he knew now, he could change the whole destiny of the valley. Conversely, if these dark secrets were kept a little longer, complete control of the valley, of Arrow and Big C alike would be firmly in the hands of this pair.

He struck with a jar which drove the breath out of him, striking on his back. For a moment he hung poised, and then slid and started to fall again. And stopped a second time, not more than two or three feet farther on down.

For a moment he lay dizzily, vaguely surprised to find himself alive. He was still on his back, his head somewhat higher than his feet, which seemed to be braced against the far wall of the shaft, with his knees bent up.

As the shock of the tumble subsided and the pain of it abated, he realized that he had not fallen far — probably not more than a dozen or fifteen feet in the first place. And apparently he was not hurt much.

The blackness had an opaque quality to it, like a substance which had been nicked or sliced at in the past without really denting it at all. It was broken only by a pale yellow glimmer of light up above. One of the pair was standing at the brink, striving to shine his candle down, but after a moment he grunted and drew back, and from the sound, Shannon knew that it was Cowles. Since Cowles, like himself, was no miner, he apparently had as little liking for such a black hole as Shannon felt for it.

The light disappeared and the murmur of voices receded and died away. Shannon explored cautiously, moving his head, then one foot. He was lying, he decided, on a wooden beam, square-hewn, or perhaps a beam and a bit of board caught at right-angles across it. These had apparently been dumped into the shaft and, instead of falling to the bottom, seemed to have struck cross-wise and stuck.

Moving his feet cautiously confirmed and helped to explain this. Apparently a good-sized stone had fallen out of the wall on that side, leaving a hole into which the end of the beam had caught. Perhaps an out-jutting roughness or stone held it on the other side.

The width of the beam appeared to be about eight inches. That left too much space on both sides of him, but not much on which to perch. Still, he had been lucky to hit on something so near the top, rather than plunge straight to the bottom.

But an incautious movement might send him spilling on down. It was chance and the cross-board that had stopped him. Now he felt a sharp roughness under his arm, and moved a little. Getting his wrists above it instead of the cloth sleeve, he realized that it was the sharp end of a bent-over spike. Here was a bit of real fortune.

It was not easy to get the knot which tied his wrists against the end of the nail. To raise himself and work the rope without losing his balance was hard work. But by wrapping his legs about the beam on which he lay and hitching up a little he could do better, and he was gradually gaining confidence.

His arms were almost numb from being tied so long, and the knot was stubborn. He snagged himself and felt the blood running, but kept doggedly at it, remembering Lansing's promise that waste — car loads of dirt and rock — would soon be dumped down on top of him.

Now the knot was starting to loosen. He rested a moment, then held his breath. Someone was up above. Was it a miner with a loaded ore car, going to the outer chute, or one with a load to dump on him?

Apparently it was the latter. He heard it grate across the untracked ground, while two men grunted and pushed. Shannon debated wildly with himself whether to yell, or not. There was a possibility that these miners might boggle at murder, but the odds were against that. Even if they were, they might not dare risk helping a man marked for death by their bosses. Those who worked here knew that they were on a lawless job.

That was one angle. He weighed it against

the thought of being swept off and knocked to the bottom of the shaft if he kept still. While he hesitated, he heard Lansing's voice.

"We want this hole filled, boys. It's risky, leavin' it any longer. Dump 'er in."

To call out now would spoil any slight chance of survival which he had. But in the next few seconds a half-ton or so of rock and dirt would rain down on him —

Shannon wrenched, and his hands came free. But already the car was being up-ended.

■ ■ ■ ■

PART IV
ONE AGAINST THE
OUTLAW BAND

■ ■ ■ ■

SEVENTEEN

There was, Shannon knew, another old beam not far above him and partly to one side, for he had struck on it first in tumbling. It might, in part, serve to break the full force of the load being dumped, to divert it from him. But only in part, for he was not directly under it. He could not see to judge about that.

It was all that he could do to use his half-numbed arms, but it was a case of act now or be brushed off. Already he had wrapped his legs about the beam. Now he turned over, holding with his arms, clinging to the under side of it desperately. If he could hold on —

Such sounds as he made were drowned in the noise up above as the car began to empty. Dirt rained down, striking his fingers, a choking cloud, spilling over him, hitting him on both sides of the beam. He heard the thud of rocks striking and bounding off and down, felt the shock as the stick quivered to the impact. From the sound below, they seemed to tumble a long way.

Then, as abruptly as it had begun, the deluge was past, with more dust rising up from below. But the beam had not been shaken loose or himself dislodged. Grimly he pulled himself up until he lay, panting, on the top side again.

He waited while the dust subsided and the sound of those up above died away. But he had to get out of here before another load was dumped. If he could get out.

The darkness was a mixed blessing. He could not see the yawning hole beneath, but neither could he see anything else. Only his hands could tell what he had to know.

How firmly these timbers were wedged, and whether his movement would dislodge them, was a question and a risk to be answered together. He got hold of the timber above and pulled himself up on it, then stood up, with hands against the side of the shaft to steady himself.

On a guess, it was another dozen feet to the top. There were outjutting stones, or holes where others had fallen out, sufficient roughness to give him a chance to climb. But once he was started, there could be no turning back. And if they gave out —

The blood was getting back into his arms so that he could use them again. Shannon found a toe-hold, then an outcropping for one hand to grasp. The next five minutes was an agonizing strain. More than once he clung and groped desperately for a hold that did not seem to be available. Always he managed to keep going, and finally his hands found the edge and he pulled himself up and sprawled, too spent to move.

The sound of someone coming was a stimulus. He got up and retreated cautiously to the side, until he brought up where coats and hats hung.

Lights were coming into view, several of them and many men, talking and laughing. Apparently the whole crew was going off-shift. Which meant that they would head straight for their coats.

Shannon moved along the wall until he came to one of the exploratory bores which had been tried and abandoned. Just back in its shelter he waited. The men were excited, and now he understood why. They had been given the rest of the day off. Everybody was leaving.

That had an uneasy sound. It might give him a better chance to move around and get out of here, but there must be some reason behind it, and he had a hunch that trouble might be wrapped in the same package.

The last of the miners left, going down the tunnel which led to the canyon. After a decent interval, he intended to follow. But the first job was to find a candle for himself, or, better still, a lantern.

The blackness was absolute now. But as he started to move he heard the dim echo of footsteps and saw the faint gleam of an approaching light from down the tunnel. Somebody was coming back. Then, closer at hand, a door opened suddenly, as though someone had been in a walled-off office. From it shone the stronger light of a lantern.

Lansing stepped out, carrying the lantern. He was looking around, scowling as though suddenly suspicious. At the same moment the other man emerged from the tunnel and halted abruptly. It was Cowles.

For a moment each of them eyed the other with mutual dislike, now clearly manifest. But there was a sly triumph on Cowles' face which he made no effort to disguise, and that seemed to increase the apprehension of his confederate.

"What are you doing back in here?" Lansing demanded. His head was cocked in a listening attitude — as though he hearkened not so much for Cowles' answer as for the sounds of activity which should have reached his trained ears, but did not.

Cowles' grin was full of a cool insolence. His voice echoed it.

"I had a little business to tend to," he drawled, "That's all."

"Business?" Lansing repeated, his voice thick with suspicion. "I tend to things in here."

"You used to," Cowles corrected. "Not any more. I took the liberty of sendin' the boys home. Told 'em you said they could have the rest of the day off. They was right pleased about it. Said some nice things about you."

"*You* sent them home?" Lansing repeated, and he was wary as a stalking cat now. "What the devil do you mean?"

"I mean that you're a damned tightwad," Cowles informed him bluntly. "You been takin' out mebby a thousand dollars a day for your shares here, and not divvyin' up. Where I'd figured it was mebby a quarter of that. Then tryin' to make me think I was gettin' a good thing, havin' the ranch for my share. That's chicken feed in the long run, compared to this. If you'd been willing to take me in as a partner, like'd have been square —"

"You've got no kick coming," Lansing said

hotly. "You got the ranch for nothing. This took a lot of money to get going, a big gamble about strikin' the vein. Along with plenty of runnin' expenses which you don't have. And I kept my agreement to the letter. That's more than you seem to be doing."

"Plenty more," Cowles sneered. "You tryin' to make me think this didn't amount to much. But today I saw how I was being played for a sucker. And I don't like that sort of a deal, mister! Then when you showed me how easy it was to dump a body down that hole, where it'll be buried till kingdom come, I decided it could be *two* bodies just as well as one."

A taut silence held while both antagonists watched each other warily. The candle flickered in the faint draft of air, while the lantern gave an acrid reek of coal-oil. Shannon tensed, and his hand, groping along the wall in the dark, found a fist-sized stone and closed on it.

"You can't get away with that!" Something like hysteria bubbled for a moment in Lansing's voice and sank again as he fought for control. "How would you explain what had become of me? You can't take over a mine like this and keep it! You don't know a thing about a mine —"

"I know plenty," Cowles assured him softly. Both men wore guns in open holsters, and Shannon, knowing Cowles' ability with a revolver, understood his confidence. Lansing, it was apparent, had no real trust in his own ability if it came to a gun duel in this tomb-like place.

"The set-up's perfect," Cowles added deliberately. "The same crew will run the mine, the same as ever. Mebby it's escaped your notice that they take my orders as quick as yours? I've had sense enough to pay 'em a bonus out of my pocket, just in case! As for you, there'll be a letter opened, on your desk at your office, callin' you East for a hurried confab with the directors. Later on, I'll let it be known that I've bought control, and that you aren't coming back. Who's going to dispute me — or stop me?"

"You can't get away with it," Lansing repeated. "The Big C —"

"Hell with the Big C! They're licked now. The only man around here that I've been scared of was Shannon. I hated his guts — but I'll admit I was afraid of him. I've had brushes with him before. He's tough to deal with. But I got the breaks today, and he's out of it — and you'll roost down there with him! Well," he added tauntingly, "you got a

213

gun. Ain't you going to try and put up a fight, even? I'm giving you a chance."

Challenged, Lansing hesitated. He ran his tongue across suddenly dry lips, the gesture of a man who realizes that in such a contest he has no chance. That not merely will he stop the other man's lead, but even the pleasure of retaliation will be denied him. He was too slow to get in a single shot, and he knew it.

But he knew too that he had no choice. If he tried now, he could assume the initiative by going for his gun. While if he waited, Cowles would draw and kill him before he could even slap leather.

It was an incongruous place for a gun-fight, but neither man seemed to think of that. Lansing opened his mouth, as if to plead or suggest a more equitable partnership. Then he closed it again, the words unspoken, knowing how futile such an appeal would be. Neither of them would ever trust the other again, in any event. This was show-down.

Shannon watched alertly. He had no liking for Lansing, who had not only acquiesced in the plan to kill him but had helped in perfecting the plot. But for the moment, until this danger of entombment was past, they were both on the same side, arrayed

214

against a common enemy. It was better to fight with an ally than alone, in such a situation.

He saw that Lansing was nerving himself for the draw, and knew that he would be too slow. The contemptuous smile on Cowles' face showed that he knew it too. Shannon threw the rock.

It had been his intention to distract Cowles, to give Lansing a chance. But events could move at split-second speed, and they did so now. Lansing made his try just as Shannon started to throw, and Cowles, an old hand at gunfighting, was watching his opponent's face, reading his intention there before his hand could telegraph the same message. His own hand moved with the speed of a pouncing cat.

Had it not been for Shannon's intervention it would have worked exactly as Cowles planned. As it was, both guns seemed to explode together, and though the light flickered and wavered, and the candle was snuffed out, the room was big enough that the lantern did not quite go out in the concussion.

Both bullets were partly wild. Lansing's because he was too nervous and hurried to take advantage of the chance given him, Cowles because the rock had hit his gun arm as he fired. Now his revolver dropped from a suddenly nerveless hand, and Shannon jumped out into the open, intending to take swift advantage of the chance.

Both gunmen were startled by this unlooked-for turn of events, at the appearance of a man whom they had believed safely dead and buried. It rendered the already palsied Lansing completely nerveless for the next several vital seconds, and it gave Cowles a bad turn.

But the outlaw was a man of iron nerve and quick perceptions. For the instant he was almost helpless. His arm numbed from the elbow down, leaving him in no position to fight back against such suddenly shifted odds. But his mind was working at full speed.

Pivoting, he ducked for the tunnel. Shannon stooped to scoop up the dropped gun and hurled himself in pursuit. The blackness ahead was absolute, but he knew that the tunnel ran almost straight and level, and if Cowles could run at headlong speed in it, so could he.

The next instant he brought up with a jar which flung him back and left him breathless, half-stunned. There was a wooden door here across the entrance, which he had not suspected. Cowles had maintained the presence of mind to shut it almost in his face.

Shannon had lost the gun as he fell. Now he got unsteadily to his feet. By this time, Lansing had begun to recover from his own half-coma, induced partly by fright, and in part by finding himself still alive after the certainty of death.

"Quick!" he gasped. "If he gets through the tunnel, we're doomed!"

He reached the door, jerked frantically at it. Apparently it had been bolted on the far side. Desperately, Lansing turned back, snatched up a heavy iron bar and belabored it like a madman. The door trembled, swung open. But even as it did, an earth-shaking roar boomed from the far end of the tunnel, and this time the lantern went out in the roaring blast of the concussion.

EIGHTEEN

Shannon lay, partly dazed, while the roaring died away and the trembling of the ground subsided. The darkness now was so heavy that it seemed like a tangible force shoving, crowding at them. Out of it, like a moan, came Lansing's voice.

"We're finished — done for! This is the end."

"What do you mean?" Shannon demanded sharply. He had an unpleasant suspicion that he knew what had happened, but he was rousing again, not in the mood to admit defeat or to give up without a fight. "We're still alive!"

"We won't be for long," Lansing answered dourly. "It'd be easier if we were dead already."

"Have you got any matches?" Shannon asked. "Let's get that lantern lit again."

"Yeah, I've got some matches — but I can't move," the reply came back. "You'll have to do it."

That answer didn't make sense, considering what Lansing had just been doing. But Shannon made his way to him, and several matches were thrust into his hand. He struck one, one tiny flame almost lost in the blackness. But he found the lantern and lit it, and the light was a cheerful island in the sea of night. Then he saw what Lansing meant.

Cowles' bullet had not gone entirely astray. It had hit Lansing in the right leg, a little above the knee — a flesh wound which was bleeding considerably and becoming increasingly painful. In the first moments of wild excitement, with panic driving him, Lansing had paid no attention to the wound. But now that he had had time to rest, the rection had set in.

"We'd better tie that up to stop the bleeding," Shannon suggested, after a look at it. "Then you can manage till we get to a doctor."

"It won't do any good," Lansing protested. "We'll never reach a medico. Don't you realize what's happened. There was a charge of dynamite set and ready, to blast shut the mouth of that tunnel where it leads in from the canyon. Just for emergencies!" He groaned. "It was my idea! Now that's all closed up, and we're trapped in here!"

That was as Shannon had guessed, and the prospect was scarcely cheerful. Cowles had lost his head, of course. Sight of Shannon, alive and taking a hand in the fight when he had been so sure that he was dead, the loss of his gun, had made him panicky. So he had done the first thing he could think of to stop them, to bottle up these two who had suddenly become such a menace to him.

Had the outlaw been in a calmer frame of mind, he might not have acted so drastically. Or again he might have decided that it would be better if the mine was closed for a few weeks until he had gotten full control of the situation.

The fact which counted was that it had

been done, and not even Cowles could undo it, except in a matter of days.

Shannon found some cloth among the supplies and whipped a bandage around Lansing's leg. The one thing which they could not afford was to go to pieces. With the bleeding checked, he took up the lantern and turned toward the tunnel.

"I'm going to have a look," he said. "And see just how bad it is."

"Go ahead, but there's no chance there at all," Lansing assured him. "I planned that blast myself. It would take a good crew a week to clear a way in here again. And we can't last a day. Even if they would be coming to rescue us."

Shannon knew what he meant. Bad air would get them in a few hours. With that passage closed, the ventilation system was shut off, and the blast itself would generate gases to make a bad situation worse. A short investigation convinced him that Lansing was right about the tunnel. It had been caved in and blasted full along at least a hundred feet near the outer end. There was no escape there. And that entrance had apparently been the only exit!

He returned to the main room, thinking about that question of air. Lansing looked up apathetically, without hope.

"How was this place ventilated, anyhow?" Shannon demanded. "There must be another outlet, since you had to have circulation. If so, there's a way out."

Lansing's face lighted momentarily.

"I didn't think of that," he confessed, and then looked glum again. "But I doubt if you could get out that way, and I know I couldn't." He pointed to one of the side-tunnels. "That leads up a couple of hundred feet to the outer air. But it's too steep to climb without equipment."

"I'll have a look at it," Shannon said. Earlier, both here and in the tunnel, he had been conscious of a slight draft, but that was gone now.

The passage led inward for a score of feet, then sloped sharply upward. The hole had been made just big enough to enable men to dig it, and for the flow of air. Far up above was a faint gleam of daylight, however, and his hope quickened at sight of it. There was a way out.

But even as he looked the light was suddenly shut away. Despair washed over him. Cowles had gotten over his panic and was thinking again. Knowing of that air shaft, and forseeing the possibility that it might be used as an escape hatch, he had lost no time in making his way there to close it.

Probably he had laid a big flat stone over it. On top of that, of course, he would pile more boulders until it was impossible to move them from below. Even with a charge of dynamite, the only result would be to blast the whole thing into a slide which would plug it more hopelessly.

A cold sensation was at the pit of Shannon's stomach, coupled with a mounting panic which he had to fight against. To die in this black hole, trapped and helpless — certainly he'd never visualized such an end, even in nightmare imaginings. Yet the last possible hope seemed now to be cut off. Lansing was a miner, an engineer, and he knew these workings as well as any man alive, had in fact planned them. If he could see no chance, it looked bleak indeed.

But Shannon stubbornly refused to accept such a verdict. He'd been in some tight places before and, with a fair measure of luck, had always managed to fight his way out of them. So long as a man could fight he wasn't licked.

He returned to where Lansing waited, and explained what had happened. The news roused Lansing enough to curse his erstwhile partner wildly. Then, out of breath, he subsided hopelessly.

"He's got us," he repeated. "And I thought

I was usin' *him* for a tool!"

"If we get out of here, will you tell the truth about who he is, to the law?" Shannon demanded. "To be sure of putting a rope around his neck?"

"Will I? I'd do that even if I put one around my own at the same time," Lansing agreed, and there was no doubt of his sincerity. "But what's the use of talking about getting even? There's no chance of us getting out."

"You were saying that that hole you shoved me down in, had been dug by the Big C crew, a few years back," Shannon said, talking out loud to try to get his own thoughts in order. "If that's so, then they had a tunnel from their own workings in to here. Where is it now?"

Lansing shook his head despondently.

"There's no chance that way," he said. "That was filled up with waste and closed tight, long ago."

"But how did they get here?" Shannon insisted.

Lansing twisted around enough to point.

"Like I was tellin' Cowles," he said, unconsciously using the outlaw's real name, which was proof that he had known it all along. "The Big C vein was pinchin' out a few years back, or they thought it was. So

223

they hoped to pick it up again by going ahead to where they thought it ought to be, and their engineers were right in guessing that it should be hereabouts. I found it all right. What they did was go off along an old worked-out shaft, then dig straight down for a while. They got about to here, then went off at an angle, and then down again in that hole I showed you."

A trace of ironic humor crept back into his voice.

"They didn't find it, but by that time, followin' the vein, it was widenin' again so that they abandoned this. Their side shaft was right where this room is now. The first down-bore was over there. But they dumped that full of waste again, pluggin' it tight. The only reason the other hole wasn't filled was that it was too far out of line."

The lantern light was small in that large cavern of gloom. But looking where he indicated, Shannon could make out the vague outlines of the old hole. It had come down through almost a solid rock ceiling, then been filled again so that it was scarcely noticeable.

Dirt and rock had been so tightly packed in that it had remained in place when Lansing's crew had come along and excavated under it. Considering that, his hopes sank.

"You any idea how far up it goes, to their regular workings?" he asked.

Lansing shook his head.

"Be pretty hard to say. Maybe thirty feet, maybe a hundred. Probably forty or fifty. There's enough ground in between that we've never heard them. Though their main workings are likely way off at the side, from up there. As I say, they sunk that shaft from some old tunnel that had been worked out."

And the tunnel may have been plugged full, too, since then! Shannon thought independently. But he did not voice that thought. This was still a chance.

"Got any dynamite down here?" Shannon asked.

"Yeah. Plenty." Lansing stared at him in bewilderment. "What for?"

"I'm aimin' to set a heavy charge of it at the bottom of that plugged-up shaft," Shannon informed him grimly. "Maybe it'll shake the filling out and drop it down in here. It's a chance."

The boss of the Dusky Lady eyed him in amazement. As a practical engineer and mining man, Shannon guessed that such a wild notion would never have occurred to him. It was too impractical, too long a chance, with even greater odds attached to the attempt.

But being neither a miner nor an engineer, he was not hampered by traditional thinking. The odds were slight that it would work. On the other hand, it was a chance — one last thing that they could do in an effort to help themselves. If it failed, they would be no worse off than before.

On the other hand, even if it worked, partially or completely, it might not help them. Such a mass of debris as now choked the shaft, released, might pour down and spread out to fill this whole room and bury them at the same time. It depended on how far that hole rose up. But again they would be no worse off than if they failed to try. Death, in such a case, would come swiftly, instead of being a matter of slow agony.

Apparently the same thoughts were passing through Lansing's mind. Quite unexpectedly, he chuckled.

"Shannon," he said. "Damned if you don't get the craziest notions! There's hardly a chance in a thousand that such a thing will work. But as you point out, we've nothing to lose by trying. And if it does dump a slide down here, maybe cave in this whole place, why, there's one good point to that. When Cowles tries to open it up again, he'll have a hell of a mess to clean out! And not an engineer among those he'll have working for him!"

"That's one way of looking at it," Shannon conceded. "But I prefer to settle matters with Mr. Cowles myself. So where's the dynamite?"

He had already located a ladder, set off at one side. He carried this across and set it up under the old shaft. By standing on it, with the light of the lantern in one hand, it was possible to observe details which had not been visible from below. He made out that an old timber had jammed cross-wise, and it had helped to hold the whole packed mass intact.

That might well prove to be the trigger to loosen it all. Beside it was a hole where some of the dirt had fallen out, a big enough place and convenient for the dynamite. He climbed back down, and found the explosive inside the office where Lansing had been at work while Cowles took over the running of affairs. Inside the small room were caps and fuses and anything else which might be needed.

Selecting several sticks, he had Lansing arrange them properly, so that he would have only to shove them into the hole and light the fuse. This would be a heavy charge, for it would be possible to try only the one time, and that might as well be a good one.

Shannon refused to think beyond the point of setting if off. If this didn't work — well, likely he wouldn't need to do any more thinking in that case.

Lansing watched, interested despite himself as the charge was placed and the fuse lit. Shannon descended the ladder again and carried it off to one side, then aided his companion into the edge of a side-shaft. They could see the faint gleam of the fuse where the flame worked along it like a creeping firefly.

The waiting was hardest. Then it came. Shannon had been prepared for a terrific, deafening thunder. Somehow the resultant explosion was an anti-climax. It was loud, but scarcely more so than the one which Cowles had set off at the tunnel mouth. The lantern went out in the concussion, the earth around them seemed to rock as if pushed by a giant hand. Then silence.

Hope ebbed out of Shannon. Nothing had happened.

Nineteen

Apparently the fill of dirt and rock had been too tightly packed in the old tunnel to be shaken loose. Only a few pieces had fallen. Lansing muttered something unintelligible, and Shannon fumbled for a match to relight the lantern. He was scratching it to flame when it came.

There was an earth-shaking rush as the piled-up tons of debris let go, as though it had been holding its breath for a moment before taking the plunge. It came tumbling, and the force of the fall was awesome in the heavy dark. Dust boiled at them in a stifling cloud so that breathing was difficult. Small stones rattled, then fell to silence.

With shaking hands Shannon tried another match and got the lantern lit, while Lansing, beside him, swore in a sort of awed undertone. The dust was so heavy that it was impossible to see much except its swirl, but out before them, its edges reaching almost to their feet, was a great pile of dirt which once had filled the shaft. It rose up like a hill, there in the middle of the room-like hole.

"I'm going to have a look," Shannon said, and climbed, with the lantern. He reached the top, and found that it was only about four feet below where the bottom of the old shaft now yawned. Looking up, he could see nothing but darkness, but the original tunnel walls had been cleaned of the waste.

"At least, it worked," he muttered, and went back down to where he had left the ladder, carefully out of the way. In the foggy light, the face of Lansing showed hope for the first time.

"I don't wonder that Cowles was afraid of you," he exclaimed. "You just don't have sense enough to know when you're licked!"

Shannon grinned faintly and tugged the ladder to the top of the pile, shoving it on up the shaft as far as it would reach. He set the base firmly, then climbed. This had worked as well as he had dared hope, but getting on out might still present a lot of problems. It looked to him as if this hole went on up for a considerable distance beyond where the ladder would reach. And what might be at the top remained to be discovered.

Then his pulse quickened. From somewhere up above came the excited sound of voices. He shouted, and a gleam of light appeared, grew stronger. Suddenly a lantern was thrust over the side, twenty feet above his head, and a face peered down, incredulous and unbelieving.

"I told you it was over this way," the holder of the lantern declared. "Hey, what's going on?"

"Can you throw us a rope?" Shannon

asked. "There's an injured man down here."

"Take it easy," another voice adjured. "They'll be from the Dusky Lady, bustin' through this way. Maybe it's a trick."

"I've got Lansing, the boss of the Dusky Lady here, all right," Shannon informed them. "He's hurt. But I'm Tom Shannon — not the man who's been on my ranch, either. There's just the two of us."

After a little more consultation up above, it was decided that there could be no harm in complying. These were miners of the Big C, of course. They had heard the roar, and had set out to investigate. Presently a rope came down. Shannon had aided Lansing over to the ladder in the meantime, and he adjusted the noose under his arms so that he could be pulled up.

"Can I count on you to clear me?" he asked. "And tell the truth about Cowles? Your chance to steal any more from the Big C is finished, in any case. But if you go through for me, I'll give you a break. You can stick to that story that you were just the superintendent, and claim that Cowles was the real boss. That will be more'n half right, anyway."

"That's treatin' me better than I deserve, after the way I've acted today," Lansing said emotionally. "But don't worry. I'll go all the way to see that Cowles gets what he deserves."

The rope was adjusted now, and those up above hoisted him up, then lowered it again for Shannon. There was increasing excitement up above, particularly as Shannon's claims were verified.

As they moved back, along a now seldom-used tunnel to the main workings of the Big C, the word had raced ahead of them. Lansing was being carried, since the wound in his leg made walking exceedingly painful. But they assisted him cheerfully, knowing that at last the secret of how the Big C had been robbed was about to be revealed.

Daylight showed ahead, and open air, with sunshine still outside. Shannon drew a deep breath. Down in those depths he had never dared quite hope to see the sun again. It was strange to think that this was still the same day. It seemed like a long time since he had descended into those murky depths.

As they stepped out into the sweetness of fresh air, a voice exclaimed at sight of them. It was Ned Files, and with him was the superintendent of Big C, as well as the "Counselor-at-law," Desseltyne.

"Under that dirt, Tom, you make a convincing replica of a miner yourself," Files said admiringly. "And I'd be willing to give long odds that you've been burrowing and come up with something that's going to be a headache for our adversaries!"

"I had some suspicions," Shannon conceded. "So I got to prowling around on the other side of these hills. With the result that I got into trouble, but it led me — maybe dumped me would be the right word — right into the Dusky Lady. Cowles figured to dispose of me. And, since some things that he wanted were too strong for Lansing's stomach, he aimed to get rid of him too. But we managed to break out into the Big C. You'll lose no more ore, Balbriggan."

Explanations were given. Amazement mounted as the others learned how the Big C had been systematically looted, via the canyon. Lansing readily confirmed that the bogus Shannon was actually Cowles, with a long record of outlawry, though supposedly dead and buried in another state. Beyond following Shannon's suggestions, he made no effort to defend himself or the part he had played.

Shannon was impatient of the time taken by all this talk. The others would want to go back inside and see for themselves, and he had no objection to that. But in the meantime Cowles was still at large, a man who had received a bad scare. If word reached him of the escape of Lansing and Shannon, after he had been certain that they were finally bottled up, he would be desperate, a mad dog let loose.

"My horse is on the other side of the mountains, and right now there's no quick way to get back to it," Shannon explained. "Have you one handy that I can borrow, Balbriggan?"

"A dozen, if you want them," the owner of the Big C assured him. "After what you've done today, Shannon, you can have anything of mine that you want, any time. Even to half of my mine, to paraphrase the old boys who used to offer half of their kingdom. Even then, I'd be better off than I was before."

"I think I'll stick to cattle, if it's all the same to you," Shannon grinned. "I've had enough of the inside of a mine to last for a long time. But I'll take the horse."

The Kid walked in a daze of blinding pain for the first few minutes. It hurt him to breathe, to take each individual step, but he was scarcely aware of that because of the greater mental agony which seared him. He had not only failed in what he had tried to do, but through his actions he had gotten the Boss into a desperate situation — one which might, as Andy knew only too well, lead him straight to his death.

Forgotten was his jealousy in this larger dilemma which involved both of them. The Boss had come to his aid when he was called. The thought that he had helped trick Shannon into a trap made the Kid squirm. His loyalty was now selfless, all to Arrow.

So wrapped up in gloom was he that at first he failed to note that the former driver had hesitated, then turned around and started back the way they had come. It had occurred to him that the best way would be to leave the Kid with the guard, at the point where the canyons formed a V. Then he could go after saddle-horses.

Andy lifted his head at sight of the guard, and understanding came to him, knowledge of where he was. It was not far from here to where he had left his horse. If he could get to it and go after help, for Shannon —

The notion fired him, driving the fog from his mind. He saw that the two were conferring, paying scant attention to him. He had been so crushed and helpless that it did not occur to them that he might try to cause trouble.

But the holstered butt of the guard's revolver was temptingly close at hand. The Kid hesitated for a moment at the boldness of the notion, then he reached and helped himself. His voice rose shrilly, threatening to break.

"Stick 'em up, you two! And be quick about it! Reach, damn you. I'd enjoy shootin' a few skunks."

Startled, they obeyed. The wildness in the Kid's face, the way his finger seemed to twitch beside the trigger, was frightening. Andy gestured with the gun.

"You're so good at tyin' a man's hands, mister, get somethin' and tie *him!* See that you do a good job. But I'll take his gun first."

He did so, then watched while his orders were obeyed. Ordering the one man to be off down the canyon, he contrived to tie the driver's hands also and start him off in the same direction. The effort made him gasp as though a knife was being driven into his side, but now they wouldn't be able to hinder him. Dropping the extra guns into a snow bank, the Kid stumbled to where he had left his horse.

It took all his resolution to drag himself into the saddle, and the jouncing was as bad as walking had been. But he pushed his cayuse at a steady trot. It would take too long to circle up-river again and back down on the far side, besides adding many miles to the ride. So he headed straight for Thunder River. His horse hesitated at the brink of the flooded stream, but the Kid spurred and swore at it, and his will prevailed.

Upstream, where he had crossed earlier in the day, it had been possible to follow wide shallows so that the horse did not have to swim at all. A time or so it had been necessary for the Kid to lift his legs to keep his boots dry, but that had been the worst. Here it was no such story. The river ran deep and swift, with considerable drift upon its current, part of that broken cakes of ice. Almost at once the cayuse was swimming, and the frigid bite of the water struck through flesh like a knife.

A couple of times the Kid thought that his over-burdened beast would founder. He knew that he ought to slip out of the saddle and cling to its tail, to give it a better chance. But he knew too that if he tried that he would never get back on, so he clung with gritted teeth and a half-forgotten prayer on his lips, and discovered finally that they were out on dry land again.

Now the wind knifed in its turn through wet clothes, but he was past thinking about that, almost past feeling. He did rouse enough when the Arrow was reached to explain what had happened. Then George was carrying him in to the house, and Pansy was helping put him to bed. While Thad Gormley made a quick examination and instructed them what to do until he should return.

George and Pansy had to stay behind to look after him. Everyone else was going, including Nancy, who buckled on a gun, her face set in white strained lines. Thad Gormley, having made sure that Andy would be well enough for a while, raced to sling his own saddle on a horse. About to mount, he paused at the shrilling insistence of the squirrel which raced toward him, protesting. He mounted, and it jumped to his boot, raced up to the saddle and ensconced itself triumphantly in an overcoat pocket. There, while it popped out its head to view the world, the medico followed where the others already spurred.

TWENTY

Bill Pesky listened, grave-faced, to Shannon's sketchy account of the happenings of the day. The sheriff had a shrewd suspicion that, had he not happened to be riding there in the street when Shannon came along, the cowboy would not have stopped. The man

238

from Arrow seemed in a hurry.

"So that's the how of it, eh?" Pesky nodded. "I've had me some long suspicions about those mines for quite a spell, but they didn't stretch half far enough, seems like. That's usual the way. You get the facts on some o' these things, and the trooth puts a man's wildest imaginin's in the shade. . . . But if you're huntin' Cowles now, why, you won't mind me sidin' you, eh? I kinda of got an interest there too."

"Be glad to have you along," Shannon agreed, and they started to turn their horses. But before they could do so, the clerk of the court came hurrying, hatless, his scanty hair flying.

"Can you come right away, Bill?" he demanded. "I was just to his house to see the Judge, and he's better. Askin' for you, kind of urgent. And, uh — he was lookin' out the window just now, Mr. Shannon, from his bed. Saw the two of you. Said he'd like for you to come too, if you would."

Shannon hesitated. He had been the first to bring the news of events to town, so it was impossible that Weldon could have heard it. And he was in a hurry. But the sheriff nodded.

"Sure, we'll come," he agreed. "I'd like it right well if you'd take the time, Shannon.

Since he wants you. Me, I — well, I'd sure appreciate it."

The sheriff's spirits had been low enough to crawl under the hump of a caterpillar. He had blamed himself keenly for losing his temper and berating his old friend as he had done. The doctor had been less encouraging. A stroke was a stroke, he pointed out. How bad this one would prove to be, he had no way of knowing, but he shook his head as though he feared the worst. Pesky had sworn softly.

"Calamity howler," he had adjured the man of medicine, but under his breath. "Always croakin' just like a crow keepin' out of gunshot!" But his own sense of guilt had been increased. If he was responsible for the judge's seizure —

Now he led the way, half-eager, half-diffident. To his surprise, Judge Weldon was sitting up in bed, a trace of color in his cheeks, his eyes almost feverishly bright. He had lain unconscious for many hours, but it appeared that, having come out of the coma, he was far from being counted out. He wore a startling red and green checked dressing gown with pale yellow splashes, which was an affront to the eyes. Bill Pesky stopped to squint, peering from under one hand.

"Me, I was thinkin' I saw the sun come up a spell ago," he ruminated. "Or has somebody been spillin' fried eggs? Where'd you get that there nightgown, Bill Weldon?"

The judge bristled, then came surprisingly close to a smile.

"This ain't a nightgown!" he denied, in a voice surprisingly strong. "If you wasn't a mossy-backed old hannyhan that didn't know the usages of —" suddenly his voice broke. "Bill!" he said brokenly. "Bill Pesky!"

"You're a durned old ranny yourself, but I'm glad to see you chirkin' up," Pesky declared, and took the judge's extended hand in both of his. Shannon detected a glint of tears in the eyes of both, and started to turn toward the door. But Weldon's voice stopped him.

"Wait, Shannon," he called. "I'd like to have you stay." He recovered his hand, fumbled under his pillow for a handkerchief, and blew his nose like a bellowing cow. "I — I want to apologize, to both of you. And to — to try and explain, Bill. I —"

"I'm the one to apologize," Pesky protested. "After the way I run off at the mouth the other day, and knowin' like I did that you wan't well —"

"It was what I had coming — what I needed," Weldon said grimly. "It took that

241

to wake me up. I'll admit that it kind of floored me at the time, but since I've had a rest and kind of got some of that load off my mind, I feel a lot better. The doctor says I'll be all right, which amazes him and maybe doesn't exactly please him. Against all the rules, I guess. But there's plenty that I've got to talk about, to really get it off my conscience. That's why I wanted to see both of you."

"You sure too much talkin' won't hurt you?"

"Do me good. I — hang it, Bill Pesky you were right. I — I've been an unjust judge. After all these years of integrity, I did sell out! It's been killing me, Bill. But I — I had to do it."

"You figured it had somethin' to do with Louise?" Pesky said gently, and it was more a statement than a question.

"How did you know?" he asked.

"We been good friends a long spell, Bill. Get it off your chest."

"Yes, we have been good friends. You're about the only one of the bunch that stuck to me when I — when I went crazy," Weldon said huskily. "Well, I — I never used to believe in messages — from the dead, or any thing like that, Bill. But since Louise died —"

"You figure you've gotten some — from her?"

"I *have* gotten some," Weldon said quietly. "Several times I've heard her voice, plainly. Usually at night, but sometimes when I was out alone, walking or riding. She sounded so — so life-like. And she told me that I was to do — to do certain things, so that she could rest easily. That's why I've rendered every decision in favor of the Dusky Lady mine, regardless of the law in the case, or of justice." He looked suddenly at Shannon.

"Whether you're the man you claim to be, of not, I don't know," he admitted frankly. "But I'm inclined now to think that you must be, because you remind me a lot of your uncle, both in looks and in your way of doing things. And I know well enough that the man on Thunder River Ranch is a scoundrel. Even though he did present the proper credentials and all that."

"That part's all right, Judge," Shannon said. "I understand."

"I doubt if you do, either of you." Agony washed across Weldon's face for a moment, travail of the spirit rather than the flesh. "I don't know how to tell you — either of you, so that you'll understand. But I — well, the voices suggested to me that maybe Louise

243

wasn't actually dead, after all, but in a state of — oh, I don't know!" He made an impatient gesture.

"I know it sounds crazy, when you actually put it into words. But I — I almost convinced myself that I — that I might see her again, some day, if I did as she said. I realize, I have all along, that it's insane. But when you hear the voice of one you love, and feel that it's her voice — well, a man, an old fool like me, will clutch at any straw. He'll sell his soul — and honor, if need be."

They were silent, half appalled by the intensity of his confession. The judge was breathing heavily, but he was not done.

"I even — thought I saw her, once," he whispered. "It was so real, Bill — I could almost reach out and touch her! That's why I've gone crooked. Though when I stop to think, I know that she would never want me to do anything dishonorable. She never was that way at all. And so — it's been driving me crazy —"

"Don't take it too hard," Shannon suggested quietly. "I think that you did hear her voice — and see her. It was in the storm, the other day, wasn't it? After she got off the stage?"

Weldon stared, his eyes bulging. His face lost its touch of color.

"Wh-what do you know about it?" he gasped.

"I happened to be where I could see the stage," Shannon explained. "I think that had been planned after the storm started, when it was figured that hardly anyone would be around to see it. I saw her get off, and saw you coming down the street. You called to her —"

"Yes! But if it had been her, she would have looked at me — or spoken," the judge gasped. "And she didn't! I knew then that I was crazy, really insane —"

"You weren't crazy," Shannon denied. "I saw her too. So did Slim Moffet, and he used to know her. Take it easy, and we'll iron this out," he added calmly. "You did get a mysterious message, telling you to be there at just that time, and that you might see her, didn't you?"

"Yes. Yes, I did. But how did you know?"

"Ever work a jig-saw puzzle, Judge?" Shannon was desperately impatient to be gone, but he steadied himself to take it easy. The health of the judge, perhaps his life, depended on a few extra moments now.

"What's that got to do with it?" Weldon demanded impatiently.

"Just this. It takes a lot of pieces, fitted together, to build a picture that makes any

245

sense. That's the way things have been here in this country. But the pieces are starting to fit together now, and I think I can see how they're shaping up. You won't need to worry about the deal I got, or the tangle with the Big C. Both of them have been straightened out, and it won't be held against you. Lansing of the Dusky Lady has admitted that this man on my ranch is a badly wanted outlaw named Cowles, and that the whole deal, mine and ranch together, was a frame-up."

Pesky was sitting quietly, waiting for him to do the talking. Weldon stared, as if hypnotized.

"But about Louise —" he whispered.

Shannon hesitated. There was still a lot of guesswork here, and he did not want to get the judge's hopes too high, only to have them dashed again. But it seemed the only way that the pieces of the puzzle would fit together.

"What I've got to say, Judge, is more or less guesswork," he explained. "Maybe I'm wrong, in part. But the man who claims to be me was shot and killed and buried three years ago, down in Abilene, Texas. I saw him dead and buried. Just the same, he's here today, alive an' well. Does that suggest anything to you?"

246

"You mean — ?"

"I mean that Cowles faked it — with the help of friends, of course. He was bad shot up, no doubt of that, and left for dead. But he got well. Somebody else was buried in his place, so as to give him a fresh start under a new name. Seeing how well it worked in his case might have given him the idea."

"The idea — ?" Weldon repeated, helplessly.

"*I* was bad shot up, too, this winter, and left for dead," Shannon said grimly. "Thad Gormley found me, like I told you, and nursed me back to life. He's a mighty good medico, one of the best. And he loved your daughter — wanted to marry her. It don't make sense, the notion that he'd poison her. I know mighty well that he didn't."

"I'm beginning to see what you're driving at," Weldon said quietly. "Go on."

"Cowles, who has claimed he was me, and Lansing, are both men with crooked records. Lansing told me all about that part of it today. They wanted the Big C ore, and they had to have control of two things to work their scheme. One was Thunder River Ranch. They worked that. But they couldn't have gotten far either way if they couldn't keep *you* under control as well. So as I

247

figure it — and here's where I'm guessing — they set out to make sure of you. Somebody managed to slip your daughter knock-out drops when Gormley was doctorin' her. Then they set up a howl that she was dead, and because he could mighty soon spoil that if he had another look at her, they got a mob worked up and rode him out of town on a rail! Though they made everybody, even him, think that she was dead! And of course there was a funeral."

"But you don't think — ?"

"I think she was just drugged. And an empty coffin buried. My notion is that she's been held prisoner all this time on Thunder River Ranch, which was another reason why they had to have it. I saw her get off the stage, the same as you did. So did Slim. I figure it was Louise."

"But — good Lord —" the judge was breathing heavily. "She never even looked at me —"

"Of course not. She's had to do these things to save your life — and her own as well, naturally. But it's fear for you that has kept her in line. If she tried to run to you and tell the truth, somebody would have put a bullet in your back! We're up against an unscrupulous skunk, in a big deal. Lansing's been taken care of, but the really dangerous man, the man with the brains, is still at large. And that's why it's time to be getting out to Thunder River without wastin' any more time, Sheriff. Up to now, I figure that Louise has been well-treated, because she's been useful, and might be worth a lot as a hostage if it comes to a show-down.

"But he's going to be like a wolf with rabies as he sees everything going to pieces, just when he thought he was set to take over this whole country. Keep your courage up, Judge. If she's alive, she's still worth a lot as a hostage. And we'll be doing our best, don't worry about that. Ready, Bill?"

"Ready," Bill Pesky agreed. "You get well for when we bring her back for a big reunion sort of a party, Bill Weldon. All right, let's ride."

TWENTY-ONE

Panic had swept Cowles for a moment. A sort of nameless fear which was worse than physical terror. Once more Tom Shannon had turned up to frustrate his plans, had come back as it were from the dead. Sober common sense assured Cowles that this was not actually so, that he had once more been mistaken and Shannon far from dead to begin with.

But reason had not come immediately to his rescue. For the first few moments, in unreasoning fear, he had chosen rather to believe that the man was dead and that his ghost was what was actually prowling these winter ranges, a fleshless nemesis against which bullets or even the deeps of a cavern had no effect. What haunted him now was a thing which would pursue him in turn to the grave. Under the stimulus of that sickly terror he had set off the blast to seal the entrance to the mine.

Once that was done, reason returned. He had simply been mistaken, of course, in supposing Shannon dead. The man was a nemesis, no doubt of that, but he was simply determined, crafty, hard to kill. This time, Cowles realized, he must make certain that there were no more slip-ups.

The only entrance or exit of the mine was sealed, and the two men trapped back inside could not live many hours without good air. Thought of air reminded Cowles of the ventilating shaft, which Lansing had once shown him, explaining the crude but effective workings of the system.

It was unlikely that Shannon could get out of that ventilating shaft, but Cowles lost no time in climbing up there and making sure that nothing of flesh or blood could crawl out of it. That done, he breathed more easily. He even sat down to collect his thoughts, to plan carefully the next steps which must be taken.

Lansing and Shannon were really entombed now, past any chance of working any further mischief. That left him in control, particularly since the judge was apparently down with a stroke which, Cowles hoped fervently, would finish him. Weldon had been useful, but now he would be handier dead. He, Cowles, would be the big boss now, not only of Thunder River Ranch but of the mine. If he worked it right, he could in time control this entire valley.

The need now was to take it easy, to plan carefully so that he would make no mistakes.

First, he would go to the regular Dusky Lady office and fix that letter which was supposed to have called Lansing away. He'd best be about that —

Cowles stopped, puzzled. The earth seemed to tremble under his feet, a dim but muted roaring reached his ears. *Earthquake,* he thought, and then, as it ended, a new and less pleasant notion struck him. There were old tunnels and shafts, down there, and Lansing was a mining man and a trained engineer. Were they hoping to blast a way to the workings of the Big C and so out again?

Such a possibility had not occurred to him before, and it filled him with apprehension. It seemed impossible, but stranger things had happened. He waited, climbing higher to where he could see to the valley spread out below, to the Big C mine buildings. Meanwhile he listened, but there was no following explosion.

He was just starting to draw an easier breath when several men came out of the buildings into the sunlight. There was Balbriggan, Desseltyne, Files — Cowles caught his breath. That man with them was Shannon.

There was no doubt about it. Again the long chance had worked, and his nemesis was still on his trail. Cowles' legs felt rubbery. Moments before, he had been finally certain that he was victor. But here was disaster.

Ruin, in fact. He did not delude himself that Lansing would not already have told what he knew. After the way he had tried to murder the owner of the Dusky Lady, Lansing would spill the whole story. With victory within his grasp, the mine and the ranch had been swept away.

Cowles stood up, cursing. It was not so

far but what he could have put a bullet neatly into Shannon, if only he had a gun. But Shannon had spoiled even that for him, making him drop his gun in the depths of the mine. All that remained now was to get away.

His mind was working again as he turned. There was time enough. This range of mountains was between the two of them, and Shannon would be forced to go down the east valley to Vermillion and then up Thunder River Valley. Whereas by going straight through the pass on the strip of Arrow ground, he would be at the ranch house long before Shannon or anyone else could get there. Time enough to get what he needed — what he wanted.

His crew would stick with him. Cowles had picked them carefully, and they were loyal, as such men went. In addition, if he fell, there would be no safety for them. They, like him, were wanted men. He'd get supplies, money — he had a lot of that there, drawn from the bank and from the sale of stock, laid up against just such a possible need for flight.

And he'd get the girl. The judge's daughter. Until escape was certain, she would be a valuable hostage still. After that — well, if he married her, the judge would use his influence for a son-in-law, to get back a daughter from the grave. So one thing at a time. He could still plan, and there was time to execute.

He'd head north, through the pass on the Arrow, on up river into the deeper mountains. Escape. It could be worked. There would be ample time.

Neither Shannon nor the sheriff cared to waste time in rounding up a posse. They were men accustomed to doing things, to trusting in themselves. Besides, a posse, while of help in certain respects, might as easily prove a hindrance here. They rode together, two silent men.

Nearing the ranch buildings, Shannon made a discovery. Off at the regular feeding grounds many of the cattle were visible. The Thunder River brand could be read easily enough. But mingling with them were a lot of cattle who disported the Arrow. Shannon shook his head in unwilling admiration.

"He did the one thing I didn't figure on," he conceded. "He brought that herd straight across the river and mixed them up with the cattle over here. He's dangerous because he always takes the boldest course. And usually nobody figures on that sort of a play."

No one was with the cattle, however. No one seemed to be anywhere around, but they moved warily, fearing a trap. Since Cowles must figure that Lansing and himself were dead and that he was now unquestioned boss in this country, he would be there. Shannon was sure of that.

But there was nobody there. They found the corrals empty of riding stock, the barns echoing, stripped of saddles. Moving more quickly, they looked in the bunk house, and it also showed signs of a hasty departure. Shannon ran for the big house, the sheriff panting at his heels.

Inside were the same evidences of abandonment. Valuables had been taken, everything else was left in disarray. On the second floor Shannon found a heavy door, ajar now, with a heavy lock which was also open. On up stairs to the garret, remembering the lights which had blinked so mysteriously from that remote window near the sky.

Here was proof of his guess. There were two big, comfortable rooms, close under the roof — rooms which a woman had occupied. Hairpins on a dresser, a comb and many other small articles added their mute testimony. There was only the one window, with iron bars across it. The house was empty.

They eyed each other in consternation. Somehow, Cowles had discovered that the jig was up. He would be heading north — and with a good start, and Louise Weldon as a hostage, the outlook was suddenly not a good one.

"I'll keep on his trail," Shannon decided. "You better go round up a posse, Bill. It'll be a long hard chase."

Shannon followed the plainly marked trail which led on north. There was no question as to where Cowles was heading. He would take the pass through the Arrow strip, cross Thunder River on up above, where Shannon had that morning, then head on north into the deeper wilderness.

It was a good plan. With several hours start, which the trail showed that they had, and a tough crew backing him, Cowles figured to be safe. The snow still lay deep in the higher mountains up river, but it was melted sufficiently that they could get through. Once far enough along to lose themselves in those fastnesses, they could separate and scatter to the four winds.

If overtaken, they could put up a hard fight. Having the judge's daughter as a hostage vastly strengthened their position.

Otherwise, Shannon had won. But if Cowles got away, and Louise Weldon was not saved — the woman whom Thad Gormley loved — it would seem to him that he had failed after all. And, so long as Cowles remained alive, he would continue to be a menace to Shannon's very existence.

Shannon was nearing the pass when a bullet whined so close to his ear that he could hear its vicious buzz.

Instantly he flung himself off his horse running for the shelter of a clump of rocks not far away. Two more bullets tried to stop him before he could reach cover, but they were not quite so close.

Startled, Shannon took stock. He had taken it for granted that Cowles, with his small army, would be hours ahead. That he would fort up here was past credence. But maybe he'd left just one or two men to hold up pursuit. He should have thought of that.

But now there was gun-fire from ahead, on the far side of the pass, guns which were answered by others in these heights. In sudden wild excitement he understood. A crew on the far side of the pass, holding up Cowles and his men. And that bunch must be from Arrow!

Just how it had come about was not important. What counted was that Cowles' plan had gone astray, and he was cornered. Though in this instance cornered did not necessarily mean trapped.

The others must have come along just in

time to force them into forting up here. To turn back down river was impossible, for Vermillion lay athwart the road.

By picking his route, crawling on hands and knees, he could reach the main pass itself, Shannon saw. Since the Arrow men were on the far side, most of Cowles' men would be watching over there as well. They would be on the heights on both sides of the pass.

Alone, it would not be so hard to keep out of sight as he moved and climbed. With luck, he might discover where Louise was being held. If he could, then Cowles would be somewhere close. It was worth the risk.

For the next half hour Shannon progressed slowly, taking advantage of every bit of cover, rock and bush and gorge. By going with infinite patience he was able to discover where the watchers were posted, without seeing him. Querulous complaints from among the crags testified to their unease.

Occasional tentative shots sounded from the far side of the pass, or droned down from where Cowles' men were forted among the steeply rising ledges. Nothing to do much damage. Up to now, both sides had been feeling each other out. Shannon had located the hiding-places of most of the gunmen, and he knew where Cowles was, still some distance above him, but on this same side of the pass.

Another half-hour of this patient stalking, climbing, inching ahead, Shannon estimated, and he would be in a position to take a hand in the game.

The strain of it was beginning to tell on Cowles' crew. They had not figured on being cornered, and the certainty that a posse would soon be along made nerves ragged. Shannon's own vanishing act, he hoped, would be having a similar effect on Cowles.

Only the fact that they were all in this situation together, and that they had a bargaining position, held them steady. Once darkness came, and it wasn't far off now, Cowles would figure on making a break.

Some one exclaimed in hushed accents. The posse was coming in sight.

The outlaws did not make the mistake of firing on them, except for a warning shot. That caused the posse to halt momentarily, then advance more slowly and warily. But this was a time for parley, and Cowles knew it. He entrusted that part of the job to one of his men, not moving from his own position. Though the confab was held a considerable distance away, Cowles could hear every word. So could Shannon.

"Reckon you know that Judge Weldon's

daughter is alive, and that we've got her," the emissary informed Sheriff Pesky without preamble. "She's been well taken care of, all these past months, with a colored maid to wait on her an' keep her comp'ny, and all. But whether you get her back in that shape, or dead, is up to you. We'll make terms, but you'll have to do the same."

"What you got to suggest?" the sheriff asked mildly.

"Just one thing. Give us your word to let us go, and the bunch of you are to stay here. That means you and your posse, and the crew of Arrow. We'll keep travelin'. And when we're a safe day's journey ahead, makin' sure that you're keepin' your part of the bargain, we'll start the girl and her maid back on horses."

Knowing Bill Pesky, Shannon was confident that he would agree to no such terms. If for no other reason, it would be because he did not trust Cowles, who had already demonstrated that his word was worthless. But Pesky would prolong the discussion, in the hope that something would turn up. While the parley went on was the time to act.

Shannon crawled a little farther, and raised his head above a barrier of rock. From here, as he had hoped, he could see

Cowles, sitting cross-legged on a shelf of rock, back in a natural fort three hundred feet above the floor of the pass.

A cave-like projection jutted overhead. Behind Cowles was the solid rock of the hill, and a yawning dropoff was in front. But a tier of loose boulders had been piled to wall the place in. On the side away from Shannon was about an eight-foot space before the path took up again. It was a well-chosen position, easy to defend. Cowles was there, along with two of his men. Back in shadow sat Louise Weldon.

Looking closely, Shannon satisfied himself that this was the same girl that he had seen in town, alighting from the stagecoach in the storm. There was no sign of the maid.

With three to guard her in such a place, they were sure that they had the situation under control, no matter what might happen in a battle down below. If it came to a show-down, they would not hesitate to kill Louise.

Three to one, *and* the girl, made unpleasant odds. But now only some twenty feet separated him from the rampart. Cowles and his men were listening to the conference going on below, not dreaming that anyone could get this close. But this marked the limit of his own advance. There was no

261

cover to go farther.

But whatever was to be done was up to him, and it had to be now, Shannon knew. The trouble was that, even if he did manage to get one, or even two of the three, in a quick burst of gunfire, the other one would retaliate on Louise. Something had roused Cowles' suspicions, perhaps a sixth sense that his enemy was near. He moved, his eyes darting restlessly. His gun muzzle was held inches from the girl's back. Only by a slight stiffening did she give any sign that she was aware of it.

"If that's you, Shannon, don't get any notions!" Cowles snarled. "Even if you killed me, I'd take her along."

Twenty-Two

There was far too much accuracy in that threat. Shannon hesitated, not moving, but Cowles did not relax. Then, looking beyond him, across that eight-foot chasm, Shannon tensed in turn. Only his training held him rigid, giving no sign.

For on the far side, skulking in the shadows next to the cliff, was Thad Gormley. He too had climbed, crawling and worming his way with infinite skill, from the far side of the pass, with the same objective in mind.

Possibly it had been he who had made the slight sound which had alarmed Cowles, but so far they had not located him.

He crouched now, partly behind an obstruction of stone, studying the situation. His eyes went briefly to where Shannon watched, and he gestured with one hand in token that he knew where Shannon waited.

All three guards were at strained attention. The odds were more even, but nothing could beat a man's nervous finger on the trigger. But it was apparent to Shannon that Gormley had some plan in mind. From where the medico crouched, he was half a dozen feet higher than Cowles.

Now his hand moved, and Shannon saw the squirrel beside him, head cocked on one side, eyes bright with expectancy. This was the moment to intervene, Shannon decided.

"I'm right here, Cowles," he announced. "And I've got you covered!"

Cowles jerked slightly, then was steady again.

"So I figured," he agreed. "But you'd better take my terms, and quick! No matter what you try, I'll kill her, even if you get me!"

The next move was up to Gormley. It came in a flick of the wrist as he tossed a nut. It was a game which Shannon had watched him play many a time with the squirrel, both at the cabin and at Arrow. The nut would be tossed, either across the room, on to a table, or perhaps to a man's lap or shoulder. It made no difference, once the bushy-tailed pet had discovered that every man in the crew was his friend.

Instantly the squirrel would be after it in one long, graceful leap. This time the nut dropped into the crease in Cowles' big hat. In one confident jump, the squirrel had cleared the intervening gap and landed on top of his shoulder, reaching for the nut even as he came to the perch.

Cowles had been sure that he was prepared for any such emergency. But this was a situation outside his wildest calculations. The impact of the squirrel not only startled him but jarred him, so that the gun-muzzle wavered. The next instant, following his pet in the same wild leap, Thad Gormley landed on the outlaw's back.

Shannon raised up, gun menacing the other two guards, who were badly startled by the turn of events.

"Make a move and it'll be your last!" he warned.

Gormley had wrestled the gun away from Cowles in one quick twist. But Cowles was struggling, frantic with terror. He twisted backward, broke away. The next instant he was hurtling downward to the canyon floor, three hundred feet below.

Silence held of a breathless moment, while all men could see what happened. Then Shannon called out.

"Cowles is dead, Sheriff. We've got the girl, and the situation's under control. You fellows better come out with your hands up. The jig's ended."

Observing the strained, half-unbelieving look on the face of Louise Weldon, the answering hunger in Thad Gormley's, he motioned to the other two now cowed guards.

"We'll get out of here," he ordered. "You better sing out so they'll understand!"

There was no more fight left in any of the crew now that their leader was gone. All that they asked was a chance to get out of the country, leaving behind the loot which they had originally planned to take. Bill Pesky agreed without argument.

"Only see that you keep going," he instructed. "Ain't no place for you around here — 'cept in jail, if I find you hangin' around after today. Though if some of the boys diskivered you," he added meaningly, "you might *be* hangin' around!"

He grinned to where Gormley and Louise, their horses close together, were riding in the dusk toward Vermillion.

"Things are sure turnin' out good," he added. "This way, the Judge'll be chirkin' up so fast that it'll make me hump to hold him even in the rest of them checker games! And we're gettin' us back the best medico in the country. While you have yore ranch. And mebby more, for all I know. Well, see you later."

He swung his horse, following the posse back toward town. Shannon turned the other way, swinging in beside Nancy. The rest of the Arrow crew had gone on ahead. A golden moon was beginning to silver the east, to send its gleam ahead on the dark waters of the river.

They rode for a while in a companionable silence. It was Nancy who broke it.

"You know," she said. "I think Cowles was right — about one thing."

"What's that?" Shannon asked.

"About this slab of Arrow, here on this side of the river. The two ranches ought to be together. We can work them — as partners. And — and that way, I won't be losing my foreman!"

"No," he agreed, observing the glint of light on her hair, the soft curve of cheek and chin. "I'm going to be hard to lose, Nancy — from now on."

We hope you have enjoyed this Large Print book. Other Thorndike, Wheeler, Kennebec, and Chivers Press Large Print books are available at your library or directly from the publishers.

For information about current and upcoming titles, please call or write, without obligation, to:

Publisher
Thorndike Press
10 Water St., Suite 310
Waterville, ME 04901
Tel. (800) 223-1244

or visit our Web site at:

http://gale.cengage.com/thorndike

OR

Chivers Large Print
published by AudioGO Ltd
St James House, The Square
Lower Bristol Road
Bath BA2 3SB
England
Tel. +44(0) 800 136919
email: info@audiogo.co.uk
www.audiogo.co.uk

All our Large Print titles are designed for easy reading, and all our books are made to last.